Books by Russell Fox

Street Ballads

Songs & Poems 1974 - 1991

Auguries

A Book According to Catter Knopfler

Mystery Plays

*The American One-Ring Revival
Minstrel Show & Free Circus*

Goatsong

The Case of the Three Comedians

Rainville

A Novel

Librettos & Scores

The Noyes Plays

*The True History of John Humphrey Noyes
and the Oneida Community*

PARTS 1 & 2

The Salt City Playhouse

An Itinerance 1978 – 1981

5
Octavos

The Very Last Dragon
A Problem Comedy

The Death of Rumpelstiltskin
Notes for a Law Lecture

Anthology of New York State Folk Music
Volume 1: Ballads & Songs of Upstate New York

Cornfield with Crows
A True Story

APPENDIX:

The Very Last Dragon
Libretto & Score

Russell Fox

5 OCTAVOS

iUniverse books may be ordered through booksellers or by contacting:

iUniverse
1663 Liberty Drive
Bloomington, IN 47403
www.iuniverse.com
844-349-9409

Because of the dynamic nature of the Internet, any web addresses or links contained in this book may have changed since publication and may no longer be valid. The views expressed in this work are solely those of the author and do not necessarily reflect the views of the publisher, and the publisher hereby disclaims any responsibility for them.

Any people depicted in stock imagery provided by Getty Images are models, and such images are being used for illustrative purposes only.
Certain stock imagery © Getty Images.

ISBN: 978-1-6632-3451-3 (sc)
ISBN: 978-1-6632-3452-0 (hc)
ISBN: 978-1-6632-3454-4 (e)

Library of Congress Control Number: 2022900347

Print information available on the last page.

iUniverse rev. date: 01/06/2022

CONTENTS

POEMS

APPENDIX

One Sonnet

School poets, pens in shirtfront pockets, once
Played truant in the rill'd green fields, and wrote
Of lamplit streets, the town girls' glance —
Heroic'ly coupletting, like bards of old.

But now, the loves those odes immortalized
Are gone, in limb and line, unmemorable —
And time proves, too, not ev'ry white haired head is wise,
Nor are the dead all venerable.

Still, I have found, almost too late, a maid
With bunions, sups on onions, wild hair dyed —
Who, with a wisdom come of age
Can startle, laugh still, wondrous as a child.

I love you truer, leaving but one sonnet
Than to write a hundred, and to love but sonnets.

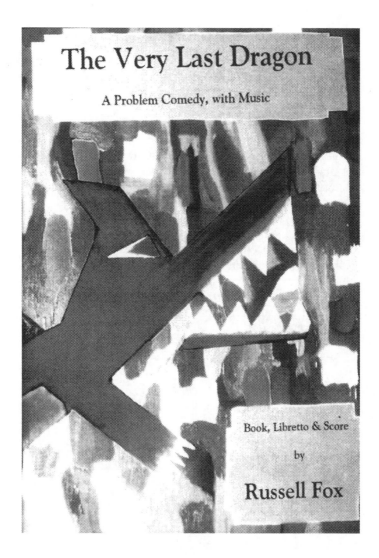

The Very Last Dragon

A Problem Comedy, with Music

Book, Libretto & Score

by

Russell Fox

The Very Last Dragon

The Very Last Dragon

A Problem Comedy, with Music

Book, libretto & score by Russell Fox

Written 1980 & 2007
Syracuse & Buffalo, New York

To my mother

Ancient Lights Books
www.ancientlightsbooks.com

CHORUS   *Including Peasants, Farmer, Soldier,*
                    Reverend, Banker

The KING

LORD HAL
LORD BURTON   *The King's Royal Ministers*

The CAREFREE PRINCESS

Her UNDERWORKED HANDMAIDEN

SAM *[later* SIR*]* SHAMBLES
SIR LESLIE
SIR QUILLIO   *Spear Carriers*

SIR ERRANT

THE VERY LAST DRAGON

S c e n e : *The Kingdom of Catatonia.*

Act One

Act I, Scene i.   The Palace Court.

Alarum: trumpets and drums. Processional music.

The Throne Room of a Castle. The backdrop is a stage-painted stoneblock wall, with a great arched window and the elevated throne before it, upstage center; tall windows palisade the two side walls.   The KEYBOARD PLAYER *enters from stage left, crouched and darting from the backstage to the piano bench, harriedly putting up the sheet music and pushing her hair out of her face and then freezing, poised, before she pounds the first chords. Enter in procession, from stage right, the fawning* CHORUS *of the royal court, anthemic:*

HARK & HAIL

CHORUS:

Hark & hail our high and mighty
Chief Executive Officer!
Tho' dark the gale and nigh the lightning
Sail on ship of state
Evermore!

Tho' the maw of death ope' wide ahead
Ever onward! Stay the course!

Hark & hail our high and mighty
Chief Executive
Officer!

The CHORUS *strews flower petals. Enter the* KING, *who is flanked by his Royal Ministers,* LORD HAL *and* LORD BURTON. *They are followed by the* CAREFREE PRINCESS *and her* UNDERWORKED HANDMAIDEN. *The* CHORUS *gathers facing the Throne as the King, majestically, sits; the* CHORUS *then proceeds offstage Left, humming the recessional. Exit* CHORUS.

Harpsichord recitativo, improvised to accompany sung dialogue in the manner of Mozartian opera:

PRINCESS: *(At a window.)*   What a beautiful morning!
                                   With the bluest of skies!
                                   Oh, I am glad
                                   That everything is so nice.

              (To the King:)   Oh, can't we go out today, papa?

KING: What are you thinking?

PRINCESS: I'm thinking of pic-nic-ing!
                                   The fields and woods, the hills and meadows,
                                   Streams and rills and *riv*-ulets!

KING: Lord Hal and Lord Burton
                                   My loyal and royal Ministers –
                                   What have you to say
                                   About a *pic-nic* today?

LORD HAL: My King, I would advise
                                   Most strenuously *against* it.

LORD BURTON: The situation in the Kingdom
                                   Most assuredly *prevents* it.

KING: *(Claps his hands.)* There you have it. No.

PRINCESS: But *why?*

Breaking glass. From offstage left, clamor and shouting, rising. Then, from outside the windows, a braying and cacophonous reprise of the anthem, almost tuneless, parodic. The KING *claps his hands.* LORD HAL *and* LORD BURTON *roll a cannon to a stage left window, point it downward, and light the fuse.* ALL *put their fingers to their ears. Flashpot explosion, the recoil of the Cannon knocking* HAL *and* BURTON *backward in pratfalls.*

Stunned silence. Then:

PRINCESS: *(At window.)* Could *that* be the reason
                         We cannot go out for a pic-nic?

KING: No!

LORD HAL: No!

LORD BURTON: No!

PRINCESS: Then why not?

KING: *(To Ministers:)*   Well?

LORD HAL: My King, you could be eaten by an animal.

LORD BURTON: Your daughter here, devoured by a beast.

LORD HAL: A pic-nic is a risky thing to contemplate –

LORD BURTON: With untamed nature waiting in the – trees.

KING: Yes! That's your answer, princess. *(Claps hands.)* Now
                   – *(To Ministers:)* What's for breakfast?

PRINCESS: Wait!
                   But all the *bad* animals are extinct, I thought.

LORD HAL: Most, but all not.

LORD BURTON: Not all, by a long shot.

PRINCESS: Well, then – What's not?

LORD HAL: Let's start with the good news.

LORD BURTON: The *progress* we've made.

LORD HAL *gestures, and a movie screen is lowered. Throughout the following a power-point presentation is projected against the screen, flicking with illustrations of the itemized animals:*

EXTINCTIONARY

HAL: Exhibit "A", the Great AUK,
A dimwitted, flightless bird,
Waddled sea rocks by the thousands
While it was clubbed and massacred.
This awkward and ungainly AUK
Nonetheless has one distinction:
'Twas the first American creature
To be hunted to extinction.

HAL &
BURTON: Now, as you know, the BUFFALO
No longer roam the plains;
The CAROLINA PARAKEET
Is but taxiderm'd remains.
The tame and trusting DODO
Was bashed between the eyes;
And the last ESKIMO CURLEW
Has been blasted from the skies.

CHORUS: The world is our res - tau - rant,
We kill and eat what we want.

BURTON: A third of all the world's FROGS
Are perched upon the brink;
The GORILLAS, off in Africa
Could follow in a blink.
The once abundant HEATH HEN
Is totally extinct;
The IBEX of the Pyrenees
Is also gone (we think).

HAL: In North America, the JAGUAR
Has been annihilated;
The KIWI of the Great Lakes
Is likewise obliterated.
The last LABRADOR DUCK
Has croaked its final quack;
The MARYLAND and NIANGUA DARTERS
Are never darting back.

BURTON: The few ORANGOUTANGS that still remain
Can now hardly be counted;
And the last PASSENGER PIGEON
Has been stuffed, handsomely mounted.
The QUAGGA of South Africa,
A zebra-headed beast,
Like the RED WOLF in America
And STELLER'S SEA COW — are deceased.

CHORUS: The world is our res - tau - rant,
We kill and waste what we want.

HAL: Now, all the types of TIGERS,
Like almost all the larger cats,
Have been destroyed or decimated
By wiping out their habitats.
The same thing can be said for
The UNARMORED THREESPINE STICKLEBACK;
And for almost every other creature
Once we melt the polar caps.

HAL &
BURTON: The VANCOUVER ISLAND MARMOT
And the WHITE RHINO, now are nixed;
Like the defunct Jamaican Monkey,
Which was called the XENOTHRIX.
The once-delicious YUNNAN BOX TURTLE,
In its shell sarcophagus,
Is as dead and gone as the ZEUGLODAN,

9

HAL: Whatever *that* was.

CHORUS: The world is our res - tau - rant,
We kill and waste what we want.
The world is our res - tau - rant,
We kill and eat what we want.
The world is our res - tau - rant,
We kill and waste what we want.

Harpsichord recitativo:

PRINCESS: If all those creatures have been nixed
Then why can't we have a pic-nic-s?

The stage darkens; portentous musical accompaniment:

LORD HAL: Alas, one beast remains
To be a problem –

LORD BURTON: The problem of the kingdom
Is the Dragon.

LORD HAL: It eats our horses in one bite –

LORD BURTON: It even eats our wagons!

Bright again; harpsichord:

KING: There you have it. We cannot have a pic-nic
When the dragon not extinct, yet. *(Claps his hands.)*
Now, I'm hungry as a horse!
What, I ask again, is for break-forst?

From offstage left, again, the clamor rises. Angry shouting, chanting to the anthem theme, this time played on kazoos. Enter stage right SAM SHAMBLES, *a Rustic, liveried as a ragged Messenger. He rushes onstage, butting and elbowing between the* KEYBOARD PLAYER *and the piano. He stands bandy-legged before the Throne, his shoulders thrown back and chest heaving, winded. When he speaks, it is with impediment: blasting his* B*'s and popping his* P*'s and spraying his* S*'s, aspirating. A sputtering bumpkin, full of earnest bombast.*

Without accompaniment:

SHAMBLES: My King! Outside the Palace, the Peasants are yelling for Bread! There's Barricades! Banners! Brigades of Renegades! They're helmeting their Heads with empty Bread-pans, and bucklering their Bodies with Sandwich Boards – with *Slogans* on the Sandwich Boards! O', my King! They're prying the Paving-stones from the Streets, and smashing them against the Castle Walls! It's *raining* pavement! Cats and Dogs! Dogs and Cats! Men in Dresses! Women in Pants!

(He takes a breath. Then:)

In short, my King, the Populace is in open Revolt!

Silence. Then, to harpsichord recitativo:

KING: Hark! What do We hear?
In the royal Ear?

A capella, without the singing:

SHAMBLES: Only the Truth, my King.

Harpsichord recitativo:

KING: What the royal Ear hears displeases us;
These unharmonious Pleas to us –

Seize the Messenger!

The KING *claps his hands.* HAL *and* BURTON *seize* SAM SHAMBLES.

SHAMBLES: *(Yelling:)*   I only told the Truth. I thought that was my job!

Harpsichord recitativo:

HAL: Your message gives offense
              Not because you had to bring it –

BOTH: No!

BURTON: The offending circumstance
              Is the fact you did not *sing* it!

> *The* KING *stands, his arms cradle-crossed. Then he gives a sharp gesture with one little finger, and* LORDS HAL *and* BURTON, *still ahold of* SAM SHAMBLES, *proceed to shove the Throne aside, so that it does not block the arched window.* HAL *and* BURTON *stand readied to defenestrate* SHAMBLES.

THE RULE OF THE KINGDOM

KING: The rule of the kingdom
              Is when words are said, to sing them –
              'Tis the first and foremost law of all the land.

              For ev'rything sounds sweeter
              Put to music, in a metre –
              Whether lowly grumble or the high demand.

              (At the stage apron, animated, tapping his toe:)

Now– if *you* plan on complaining
Just make sure you are refraining
And explaining your complaint in the refrain
For it's hard to be unhappy
To a tune that's bright and snappy
Going round and round in endless roundelay.

(He swirls.)

HAL & BURTON*:*   The rule of the kingdom
Is when words are said, to sing them –
'Tis the first and foremost law of our great King.

Even grievances sound gaily
When sung to a ukelele –
For the sharpest barb in song doth lose its sting.

KING*:*   So, if *you* should have a comment
You must put it in a sonnet
And at least have someone hum it while you croon.

For the vilest of the curses
Once set forth in rhyming verses
Can be palatable, *when* put to a tune.

ALL *except* SHAMBLES, *including the* CAREFREE PRINCESS *and
her* UNDERWORKED HANDMAIDEN, *in a vibrant round*:

ALL: The rule of the kingdom
Is when words are said, to sing them –
'Tis the first and foremost law of all the land.

For ev'rything sounds sweeter
Put to music, in a metre –
Whether lowly grumble or the high demand . . . .

Sudden stop when the KING *finishes a verse.*
Silence, then the KING, *ominously, in spoken voice:*

KING: I didn't hear you *singing.*

Awkwardly, a capella:

SHAMBLES: I'm sorry, my King . . . that I didn't sing.

Harpsichord recitativo. In sotto voice:

KING: Are you really sorry?

SHAMBLES: I'm really, truly sorry.

> *Pause. Piano underscore; the introduction to the plaintive and lovely Princess' Aria Theme:*

PRINCESS: Have pity, Father!

HANDMAIDEN: Show mercy, my King!

PRINCESS: Stay thy hand from slaughter –

BOTH: Let him live to sing!

> *The* KING *carefully considers, then claps his hands. Two* SPEAR CARRIERS *enter from the Wings and lay hold of* SHAMBLES, *taking custody of the prisoner from* LORDS HAL & BURTON, *who brush off their hands and move downstage, to the right of the* KING. *Bass drumbeat and blocked piano chords, fast and thundering; the Dungeon Theme:*

KING: Take him down to the Dungeon!
Clap him in Irons!
Let him just sit there and stew!

Put him on ice, right
Out of my eye-sight –
While I decide what to do!

HAL & BURTON: Down to the Dungeon!
Clap him in Irons!
Where he can sit there and stew!

Put him on ice, right
Out of your eye-sight –
While you decide what to do!

SHAMBLES *is frog-marched off the stage by the two* SPEAR CARRIERS. *Abrupt shift to harpsichord recitativo:*

KING: At last!
And now– What is for breakfast?

If a night performance, the stage dims and a spotlight snaps on HAL & BURTON, *who freeze in the circle of white light like vaudevillians. Ascending piano scale, glissando. Then* HAL *takes the intro.*

THE BREAKFAST SONG

HAL: On the continent, the breakfast
Is orange juice and a roll –
But a continental breakfast
Is not fit for one so roy-al.

BURTON: The French can have their toast
With spice and sugar sprinkling;
Let the English eat boiled oats –
Hardly fare fit for a King!

KING:	But, what breakfast is for *me?*
HAL & BURTON:	*A delicacy!*
HAL:	Roasted mutton is a leg Most excellent!
BURTON:	And some do say that snails and such Are succulent!
HAL:	But the Dragon has an Egg Penultimate!
BURTON:	Whether scrambled, boiled or poached Or as – An omelet!

Uptick, as the two SPEAR CARRIERS *roll in a giant Egg from the wings.*

HAL & BURTON:	One Dragons' egg roasted, Or boiled, braised, or broasted, Alone is a feast for a day! Have it soft-boiled or hard-boiled, Or sautéed in whale oil; Or dragon's egg over easy, with O.J.
KING:	Can I have a side of sausage, ham or bacon?
BURTON:	After a dragon's egg, all else will be forsaken!
HAL & BURTON:	Whether sunny-side upwards, Or baked into custards, The egg that's a feast for a day!
ALL:	The egg that's a feast for a day!

Freeze in tableau. Blackout & Curtain.

Act I, Scene ii. A Palace Boudoir

Enter the CAREFREE PRINCESS, *in petticoat, and her* UNDERWORKED HANDMAIDEN, *with a handmirror. Discarded clothes, shoes, and hats are scattered about the floor and furniture of the boudoir. Harpsichord recitativo:*

PRINCESS: *(Carefreely:)* I'm so happy that everything is so nice.

HANDMAIDEN: *(Holding a handmirror for the* CAREFREE PRINCESS, *who primps:)* I'm so happy, too. Nothing could be nicer, and we haven't got a worry in the world.

PRINCESS: What on Earth could possibly go wrong?

Piano music begins, a bouncy melody reminiscent of a children's ballet recital. Throughout the following song the CAREFREE PRINCESS, *assisted by her* UNDERWORKED HANDMAIDEN, *picks up various articles of clothing but discards most of them, gradually getting dressed.*

WHAT ON EARTH COULD POSSIBLY GO WRONG?

TOGETHER: We don't have a worry in the world,
PRINCESS: We're the freest spirits in the Kingdom.
TOGETHER: If the world's an oyster, we're its pearls,
HANDMAIDEN: We're sweeter than two sugar plums, and then some.

PRINCESS: I think tonight I'll wear this gold laced ball - gown —
HANDMAIDEN: It won't do to put just any plain old rag on —

TOGETHER: So — What on Earth could possibly go wrong?

HANDMAIDEN: *(Spoken:)*   But Mistress, don't you think—?
PRINCESS: I shouldn't think so! No! —

PRINCESS:	We don't have a worry in the world,
HANDMAIDEN:	Life's a bowl of cherries and a sweet song.
PRINCESS:	We're a pair of happy, carefree girls,
HANDMAIDEN:	For what we want, we never have to wait long.

PRINCESS:	No high-heeled shoes to catch the carpet shag on —
HANDMAIDEN:	No sharp furniture for stockinged legs to snag on —

TOGETHER:	So — What on Earth could possibly go wrong?

HANDMAIDEN:	*(Spoken:)*	But, Your Highness, what about—?
PRINCESS:		What? But nothing! No! —

TOGETHER:	We don't have a worry in the world,
PRINCESS:	We're the fairest flowers in the Kingdom.
TOGETHER:	People like to see us toss our curls,
HANDMAIDEN:	Except that sometimes people think we're ding - dong.

PRINCESS:	What a pretty hat —
HANDMAIDEN:	But dear, you've left the tag on —
PRINCESS:	How I hope this dance and dinner doesn't drag on —

TOGETHER:	Now — What on Earth could possibly go wrong?

Offstage rumbling. The music stops; they listen.

BOTH:	What's that?

Enter a DRAGON, *fearsome & snorting & smoking.*

BOTH:	*In unison:*

OH, NO! IT'S THAT NASTY OLD DRAGON!!!

The PRINCESS *and* HANDMAIDEN *panic and scream. The* DRAGON *chases them offstage. Blackout and curtain.*

Act I, Scene iii.   The Palace Court.

The KING, asleep on his throne, snores. In front of him, a table with the remains of the breakfast: the giant broken eggshell, plates and goblets and cutlery. The floor rumbles, the dishes begin to clatter, and the throne is shaken. A framed picture of a typical kingdom scene slides off the wall and crashes to the floor. The KING stirs. Enter the two SPEAR CARRIERS from opposite wings of the stage, in panic. They have a great deal of difficulty keeping their armor and helmets intact while holding onto their clumsy spears at the same time. They meet in the middle of the stage and parry frenzied, operatic exclamations.

1ST SPEAR CARRIER: An earth-quake?

2ND SPEAR CARRIER: A flash flood?

1ST SPEAR CARRIER: A mudslide?

2ND SPEAR CARRIER: A tidal wave?

OFFSTAGE   *(Terrified:)*   The Dragon is coming!
VOICES: The Dragon is coming!

SPEAR CARRIERS: *(In unison, quaking:)* THE DRAGON!

The two SPEAR CARRIERS run to a window, gesticulate. Enter HAL and BURTON, as the KING rubs his eyes and stands. The rumbling continues.

1ST SPEAR CARRIER: Your Highness!
                          The Dragon is escaping the Castle!
                          It's crashing its tail, and slashing its talons!

2ND SPEAR CARRIER: It's snorting fire and smoke –
                          It's leaping across the moat!

1ST SPEAR CARRIER:.   My King!
                          Beneath its wing, the beast doth clutch
                          The Princess!

2ND SPEAR CARRIER: And 'neath th' other batlike wing
                      Hath clapped the Underworked Handmaiden!

1ST SPEAR CARRIER:.   O' King!
                      The Dragon is making away with them!

The rumbling of the floor subsides. Silence.

Then, to harpsichord recitativo:

KING: Hark! What do We hear?
                      In the royal Ear?

A capella, without the singing:

SPEAR CARRIERS: The Dragon –

The KING cuts them short with a handclap. Recitativo, menacingly:

KING: I didn't hear you *singing.*

HAL & BURTON: *(In song:)*
                      The rule of the kingdom
                      Is when words are said, to sing them –
                      'Tis the first and foremost law of all the land.

KING: *(Handclap.)*
                      There's no time for that now!
                      Seize Them!

HAL and BURTON seize the two SPEAR CARRIERS.

DOWN TO THE DUNGEON

KING: Take them down to the Dungeon!
Clap them in Irons!
Let them just sit there and stew!

Handcuff and crack them!
Shackle and rack them!
Make sure you turn ev'ry screw!

HAL & BURTON: Down to the Dungeon!
Clap them in Irons!
Let them just sit there and stew!

Handcuff and crack them!
Shackle and rack them!
Make sure you turn ev'ry screw!

KING: This *could* be a tragedy!
I need a strategy!
Crisis, catastrophe looms!

I need better surveil-i-lance!
Suspend habeas cor-pe-us!
For toward us approaches our dooms!

HAL & BURTON: Down to the Dungeon!
Clap them in Irons!
Make sure you turn ev'ry screw!

Handcuff and crack them!
Shackle and rack them!
Torture until they turn blue!

KING: Now!

Harpsichord recitativo:

LORD HAL: Your ev'ry wish, we shall obey
                    Without a doubt, or undue delay –

LORD BURTON: But first, exalted Eminence,
                    Your subjects seek an audience.

At the behest of LORDS HAL & BURTON, *the* CHORUS *files out from behind the stage and lines up in from of the apron. Included among them are a* FARMER, *a* SOLDIER, *a* REVEREND, *a* BANKER, *and several assorted* LUCKLESS PEASANTS. *A lively piano vamp commences, the* CHORUS *and soloists chanting, led on and conducted by* HAL & BURTON.

THE DRAGON IS THE PROBLEM OF THE KINGDOM

PEASANTS: The Problem of the Kingdom is the Dragon,
              The Dragon is the Problem of the Kingdom.
              The Problem of the Kingdom is the Dragon,
              The Dragon is the Problem of the Kingdom.

FARMER: The Dragon is the Problem of the Kingdom,
              It tramples cows and crops beneath its feet.
              If it wasn't for the ugly, nasty Dragon,
              Us luckless folks would have enough to eat.

HAL &   It's the root of plague and pestilence and famine;
BURTON: The Dragon Is the Problem of the Kingdom.

PEASANTS: The Dragon is the Problem of the Kingdom,
              The root of plague and pestilence and famine.

SOLDIER: The Dragon is the Problem of the Kingdom,
              Its armored plates, like toothpicks, snap our arrows.
             We can't, with present weapons, kill the Dragon,
             Its fi'ry breath burns up our fellow soldiers.

HAL &   Its bark is worse than bites from France and England;
BURTON: The Problem of this Kingdom Is the Dragon.

PEASANTS: The Dragon is the Problem of this Kingdom,
             The root of plague and pestilence and famine.
             Its bark is worse than bites from France and England;
             The Problem of this Kingdom is the Dragon.

REVEREND: It rots the moral fibre of our children,
             Who play at games pretending they're all dragons.
             Its power and its flashy ways mislead them,
             And turn them into truants, rogues, and hoodlums.

HAL &   Its gluttony and slothfulness are wanton;
BURTON: The Dragon is the Problem with this Kingdom.

PEASANTS: The Dragon is the Problem with this Kingdom,
             The root of plague and pestilence and famine.
             Its bark is worse than bites from France and England;
             The Problem with this Kingdom is the Dragon.

             Its gluttony and slothfulness are wanton;
             The Dragon is the Problem with this Kingdom.

BANKER: As I have said in boardrooms 'cross this nation,
             The capital we'd otherwise be leading
             Is tight because collateral & business ventures pending
             The Dragon's fangs may suddenly be rending.

HAL &   It hits our bottom lines
BURTON: And pinches off our profit margins;
             The Problem of this Kingdom is the Dragon.

PEASANTS: The Dragon is the Problem of this Kingdom,
             The root of plague and pestilence and famine.
             Its bark is worse than bites from France and England;
             The Problem of this Kingdom is the Dragon.
             Its gluttony and slothfulness are wanton;
             The Dragon is the Problem with this Kingdom.
             It hits our bottom lines and pinches off our profit margins;
             The Problem of this Kingdom is the Dragon.

BANKER: As I have said in boardrooms 'cross this nation —

REVEREND: It rots the moral fibre of our children —

SOLDIER: We can't, with present weapons, kill the Dragon —

FARMER: It tramples cows and crops beneath its feet!

ALL: One Thing we all agree on:
            The Dragon is the Problem of the Kingdom.
            The Problem of the Kingdom is the Dragon,
            The Dragon is the Problem of the Kingdom.

            The Dragon is the Problem of the Kingdom.
            The Dragon is the Problem of the Kingdom.
            The Dragon is the Problem of the — KING!

The music ceases, and the LUCKLESS PEASANTS *begin to chant.*

PEASANTS: THE DRAGON IS THE PROBLEM OF THE KING!
            THE DRAGON IS THE PROBLEM OF THE KING!
            THE DRAGON IS THE PROBLEM OF THE KING!
            THE DRAGON IS THE PROBLEM OF THE KING!

The KING *tries to look dignified as the* LUCKLESS PEASANTS *continue their chanting. Ominous horns, timbrels and tabors, and a church organ underscore the* KING'S *majestic spoken delivery. Recitativo:*

THE KNIGHTING OF SIRS LESL0IE, QUILLIO, AND SAM SHAMBLES

KING: Our Kingdom has been ravaged
                        By a great and terrible Dragon!
                        It eats our horses in one bite,
                        It even eats our wagons:

> Thus, We now call for volunteers,
> The bravest in the land,
> For he who delivers the Dragon's ears
> Shall win our daughter's hand!
>
> Let those who boast that they are best,
> Stout-hearted, swift with sword,
> Step forward and accept this Quest,
> And kneel before your Lord!

LORDS HAL & BURTON *surreptitiously exit. After a long pause, the* 1ST SPEAR CARRIER, *hereinafter known as* SIR LESLIE, *steps forward.*

LESLIE: I, Leslie of Shopshire, do accept the Quest!
          (He kneels before the KING.*)*

KING: Leslie, think hard, ere you take up this test,
          How you'll handle yourself in a row.
          The Dragon's the thing at the end of this Quest,
          It isn't toothpaste, you know!

LESLIE: I know!

The 2ND SPEAR CARRIER, *henceforward known as* SIR QUILLIO, *steps forward.*

QUILLIO: I, Quillio of the Mucklands, do accept the Quest!
          (He kneels before the KING.*)*

KING: Quillio, think, ere you take up this test,
          Lest in battle you quake, pale, and sicken.
          The Dragon's the thing at the end of this Quest,
          It isn't the job for a chicken!

QUILLIO: I know!

LORDS HAL & BURTON *have unostentatiously re-entered with* SAM SHAMBLES, *who is shackled and manacled.*

25

SHAMBLES: Aw, what the Hay— as I always say —
            When I fall into thistles and brambles;
            The Dragon I'll can, and win the Princess's hand,
            Sure as my name's Sam Shambles.

            (He stumbles to his knees in front of the KING.*)*

KING: Shambles, do think, ere you rise to this test,
            Of the Dragon's great hunger and thirst.
            But with Leslie and Quillio pledged to this Quest,
            You probably shant do much worse.

SHAMBLES: You betcha!   *(Belches.)*

KING: As no other soldiers have risen to fight,
            The King of this Kingdom shall make these three Knights.

    The KING *very ceremoniously touches each of their shoulders in turn with a* sword:

KING: I dub thee Sir Leslie, The Chartreuse Knight.

            I dub thee Sir Quillio, The Lemon Liver'd.

            I dub thee Sir Shambles, The Last Knight.

SHAMBLES: *(Flinching and touching his shoulder:)* OUCH!

KING: Our Kingdom has been ravaged
                        By a great and terrible Dragon!
                        It eats our horses in one bite,
                        It even eats our wagons!

                        Now, you three are our mightiest Knights,
                        The best and very bravest;
                        So help us out of these terrible nights,
                        And slay the beast and save us!

                        Now — GO SLAY THE DRAGON!

PEASANTS: *(Taking up the chant:)*

> GO SLAY THE DRAGON!
> GO SLAY THE DRAGON!
> GO SLAY THE DRAGON!
> GO SLAY THE DRAGON!

The KNIGHTS *stand and do a smart about-face. They march to the apron of the stage, halt, and chant in chorus.*

CHANT OF THE BENIGHTED KNIGHTS

KNIGHTS: All for naught, and naught for all!
To hunting dragons we are called!
We hope it won't rain, we hope it won't snow,
Whoa, no; whoa, no.

KING
& PEASANTS: GO SLAY THE DRAGON!
GO SLAY THE DRAGON!
GO SLAY THE DRAGON!
GO SLAY THE DRAGON!

KNIGHTS: *(Turning and marching to the wings:)*

High & low, high & low,
A - hunting dragons we must go.
We hope it won't rain, we hope it won't snow,
Whoa, no; whoa, no.

ALL: GO!

Exeunt KNIGHTS.

Curtain.

Two stage hands cross the stage with a white bedsheet that has SCENE IV *painted on it. They turn and re-cross the stage, displaying the words* THE DRAGON'S LAIR *on other side of the bedsheet, and exeunt.*

Act I, Scene iv. The Dragon's Lair.

The DRAGON *is sleeping, stretched across the entrance of the* DRAGON'S LAIR. *The* CAREFREE PRINCESS *and her* UNDERWORKED HANDMAIDEN *are perched atop two gigantic eggs, prisoners. Recitativo:*

PRINCESS: We should escape now, while he's sleeping—
                     While the Dragon sleeps and dreams and snores.

HANDMAIDEN: We can't escape! Not e'en by creeping!
                     The Dragon sleeps in front of yonder door.

PRINCESS: It's been three days. I wonder why
                     That mean, ferocious Dragon hasn't feasted on us yet.

HANDMAIDEN: Don't give him any ideas, dummy!

The DRAGON *stirs. After a tense second, the* CAREFREE PRINCESS *retorts in a whisper.*

PRINCESS: Dummy?

HANDMAIDEN: Sorry.

PRINCESS: It's okay. We're under a lot of stress.

HANDMAIDEN: Thanks for understanding. You really are a princess.

PRINCESS: If friendship 'twas a custard pie,
                     Tis now the pudding's to be proved.

HANDMAIDEN: Our friendship's thick and sweet— Oh my!
                     I think the Dragon moved!

The DRAGON *raises its head, drowsily.*

PRINCESS: Whatever shall we do?

HANDMAIDEN: A lullaby! The savage beast, to soothe!

PRINCESS: Look! A guitar!

The Princess points to a guitar, in a heap of baubles and treasure.

>Oh, please sing to me the lullaby
>you sing to me, at home!

The HANDMAIDEN *retrieves the guitar, plays and sings. Piano underscore, sotto:*

BEDTIME STORY

The children have knelt at their beds,
Their prayers are over now;
And may they sleep, their souls to keep –
At least until the morrow.

>But the ghosts still speak through heatpipes,
>If you listen in the night;
>And the thieves will creak upon the stairs
>Then vanish with the light.

So sleep ye now, my Princess,
Do not listen for these things;
They are just the wind that rambles,
And the timbers settling.

>And the night does have its solace,
>For in the dark I can pretend:
>That I am with my Princess,
>And in my bed again.

Slow to Black, with the PRINCESS *and the* DRAGON *snoring.*

Act I, Scene v.   The Greenworld. Midnight, at a Stream.

SIR QUILLIO, SIR LESLIE, *and* SIR SAM SHAMBLES *sleep, or at least pretend to sleep, beside the glowing coals of a campfire. When the approaching clop of a galloping horse becomes faintly audible,* SIR QUILLIO *leaps up and throws more wood on the fire.* SIR LESLIE *sits up in panic.* SIR SHAMBLES *wakes reluctantly, annoyed. Melodramatic lute:*

SHAMBLES: What is the matter? What do you hear?

LESLIE: Somebody's coming, and coming quite near.

QUILLIO: I heard it, too – so 'tis not a dream–
            Something approaches, across yonder stream!

LESLIE: Could the Dragon be hunting for someone — Of course, us?

SHAMBLES: Try not to be silly– Dragons never ride horses!
            (Shambles goes back to sleep.)

LESLIE: If 'tis not the Dragon, beast loosed from its lair,
            Then what rides by night, by stallion or mare?

QUILLIO: If I had that answer, Sir Leslie so fair,
            My sword would be scabbarded, not ready to tear!

LESLIE: *(His voice tremor'd, lilting:)*   Could it be a terrible tiger, or bear?

QUILLIO: *(Quaking:)*   I doubt it is either – But Hark! Who goes there?

ERRANT: *(From offstage, across the Stream:)*
            How do I get across the Stream?

LESLIE: You're already across the Stream!

Enter SIR ERRANT, *who mimes riding, fords the stream and   dismounts. He looks at the two* KNIGHTS, *now cowardly pouting. His tone is conciliatory, calming, and sly.*

ERRANT: Oh, what is the matter, ye wandering knights?
           What are yer problems? yer pressures? yer plights?

LESLIE: We're questing to kill off the Very Last Dragon,
           And to tell you the truth, we fear we'll be eaten.

ERRANT: Alas, I too am hunting the Very Last Dragon,
           And, as there's no other, it must be the same one.
           For by day and by knights, the Dragons are slain,
           And the Dragon we seek's the sole one that remains.

QUILLIO: If the Dragon we seek is the last that remains,
           Then let us join forces, swap stories, give names!

Music. SIR ERRANT *breaks into song, with* SIRS LESLIE & QUILLIO
providing the backing vocals. SIR SHAMBLES *rolls over, covers his head
with a pillow. By the end of the song, the three unsleeping* KNIGHTS *are
doing a can-can dance routine.*

WHIP-SONG OF THE ERRANT KNIGHT

ERRANT: My name is Sir Errant,
           I think it's apparent,
           My business is dragons— to slay.

           And when pauper or tyrant
           Asks for my appellant,
           I look in his eyes, and I say—

           My name is Sir Errant,
           I think it's apparent,
           My business is dragons— to slay.
           I track down their nests
           And I scramble their eggs,
           Or make eggs over easy, with O.J.

LESLIE: My name is Sir Leslie,
           I wear prints of lime paisley,
           I hunt butterflies in the field.

But if some ugly dragon,
Should rap on my noggin,
To that dragon I'll cry out to yield.

ERRANT: I think it's apparent
That you're a knight errant,
Your business is dragons— to slay.

ERRANT
& LESLIE: We like dragons roasted,
Or boiled, braized, or broasted,
A dragon's a feast— for a day.

(Can-can dance.)

QUILLIO: I was knighted Sir Quillio,
Knight of the bright yell-e-ow,
And quest for my manhood— to prove

That if some dragon punches me,
Kicks me, or crunches me,
Never a nerve shall I move.

ERRANT
& LESLIE: We think it's apparent
That you're a knight errant,
Your business is dragons— to slay.

All: We eat eggs for breakfast,
Roast legs for a re-past
Of dragon— a treat any day.

ERRANT: We three are knights Errant,
We think it's apparent,
Our business is dragons— to slay.

And when peasant or soldier
Asks us our order,
We look in his eyes, and we say—

ALL: We're the Knights of the Errant,
We think it's apparent,
That our business is dragons— to slay.

Whether braized, boiled, or roasted
Or baked, boiled, or toasted
A dragon's a treat any day.

Offstage rumbling begins. The Knights *at first cock their ears, then put their ears to the ground as the rumbling becomes progressively louder.* Shambles *rouses, rubs his eyes.*

ALL: What, ho?

LESLIE: An Earth-quake?

QUILLIO: A flash flood?

ERRANT: A landslide?

Enter the DRAGON; fearsome, as before.

KNIGHTS: *(Knees knocking, in fright:)*   THE DRAGON!

Sirs Leslie, Quillio & Errant *bolt and exit, but* Shambles *conceals himself behind a piece of shaped stage flattage which has been painted to resemble a* Shrub. *The* Dragon, *a huge, green, and ugly beast, makes menacing gestures at the two retreating* Knights. *Once the* Dragon *believes itself to be alone, however, it does not need to appear fearsome. The stage darkens. Spotlight. Music begins, and the* Dragon *begins to sing. The song is mournful at first, but it soon picks up, and the* Dragon *accompanies the tempo with a sort of soft-shoe.*

The Very Last Dragon

DRAGON: What do you do when you're a dragon,
                And it happens that you are the very last?
                What do you do when you're a dragon,
                In a world where dragons are a thing of the past?

It's a weighty and a great respons-ibil-i-ty,
Needing all a dragon's wits, and its agil-i-ty-

Oh, what do you do when you're a dragon?
You drag on, and on, and on, and on, and on.

Oh, what do you do when you're a dragon,
And the dragon fam'ly's coming to an end?
You may be the one and only living dragon,
But you don't have any other dragon friends.

Now, the dinosaurs are washed up and they're his-tor-y
Because they didn't solve this very scary mys-ter-y—

Oh, what do you do when you're a dragon?
You drag on, and on, and on, and on and on.

(Interlude & soft-shoe.)

Oh, what do you do when you're a dragon,
And it happens that you are the very last?
What do you do when you're a dragon,
In a world where dragons are a thing of the past?
It's a solemn and a great respons-ibil-i-ty,
Needing all a dragon's smarts and ingenu-i-ty —
Oh, what do you do when you're the
   — very last dragon?

You drag on, and on, and on, and on, and on.

The DRAGON *finishes with a flourish and bows, perhaps reprising the second verse as an encore. When the music stops the* DRAGON *holds its pose and* SHAMBLES, *now standing up behind the* DRAGON, *takes a handkerchief from his breast pocket. He wipes a tear from his cheek and blows his nose, then ducks behind the shrub when the ensuing honk causes the* DRAGON *to rear about.* SHAMBLES *darts offstage, but the* DRAGON *prefers to bask in its applause and does not follow.*

Curtain & Intermission.

Act Two

Act II, scene i.   The Palace Throne Room.

Spotlight rises on Lords HAL & BURTON, *top-hatted, cravatted, in tails. Much rubbing of palms, back-slapping and glad-handing, vaudevillian posturing.*

ACCORDING TO PLAN

HAL: Young Hal and Master Burton,
     To finest schools were sent;
     And being duly dutiful
     To the finest schools they went

     Where they charmed all of their teachers,
     Of the bullies, not one scoffed –
     For Masters Hal and Burton
     Most promptly bought them off.

BURTON: As lads, our Hal and Burton
     Their schooldays put behind;
     And being both quite fortunate
     Struck out, fortune to find

     Establishing a partnership,
     They drew up legal terms;
     And then went into business as
     The Hal & Burton Firm.

HAL & BURTON: First, we
       Buy up all of all of the factories
       Until we have monopolies
       Then ship production overseas
       And pay the help a few rupees

BURTON: And yen! And pesos, rubles, yen!

HAL & BURTON: And then we ship the product back
And sell it on a discount rack;
And when we've picked their pockets clean –
Well then, we do it all over again!

BURTON: Again! Again and again and again!

HAL: And when we need a distraction
HAL & BURTON: That's when we trot out the Dragon!

HAL: For scores of generations,
The Dragons in their caves
Have made their habitation
From hatchlings to the grave

'Neath heaps of bones and other stuff
Are diamonds, rubies, spoils –
And if you dig down far enough
You get down to the – Oil!

HAL & BURTON: So the
Evil Dragon must be destroyed
A make-work job for the unemployed
Who get fed and shod and are then deployed
To march off into the wastes and void

BURTON: Deployed! A duty we avoid!

HAL & BURTON: And if a few come marching back
Reporting that the Dragon's whacked –
They trade their swords for spades to dig
Employed out on the drilling rig.

HAL & BURTON: Then we
Ship the oil from overseas
And pipe it to our refineries
And pay the help a few rupees
While we two dine on wine and cheese

BURTON: Such bries! Bordeaux and roquefort cheese!

HAL: From roughnecks to the depot clerks –
All need the gas to get to work;
BURTON: So when they have a buck to spend
HAL & BURTON: Well, then we sell it right back to them!

HAL: And for every thousand bucks they spend
Lords Hal & Burton get a grand!

BURTON: So great! So grand!

HAL & BURTON: And that's all according to plan!

Spotlight blacks.

Act II, scene ii.   Outside the Dragon's Lair. Dawn.

Offstage clopping, like galloping. Enter Knights, *marching in skip-step. They cross the stage to the opposite wing, turn and cross the stage again, and turn again and proceed to stage center, where they stop.*

March of the Benighted Knights

Knights:

We stomp and tromp
Through the woods and swamps,
All yelling a hearty 'HEY!'

This path we beat
With thundering feet,
To keep all the bears away!

The woods are full of
Bears and wol-oves
Hungry for a snackette!

All beasts of prey
We keep at bay
By raising such a racket!

Drumbeat, for marching:

Shambles: *(Speaking:)*   You know, we don't have to sing all the time. I
                                      mean, we're out of the Kingdom, now.

Pause.

ERRANT: *(Singing:)*

                  All pledged are we,
                  In fealty,
                  Sworn to a King, emphatic:
                  That, per our oath,
                  Our words be quoth
                  In syllables i-am-bic

LESLIE: We sing these in
                           Such a terrible din
                           That bears run from the racket!

KNIGHTS   But, if prints we saw
EXCEPT   Of a Dragon's paw –
SHAMBES: We're duty bound to track it!

DRAGON: *Low, thundering roar.*

QUILLIO: Hark!

LESLIE: What?

QUILLIO: Hark!

ERRANT: What?

QUILLIO: Hark, I say!

SHAMBLES: *(Shrugs)* Okay, already.

ERRANT: *(Ear to the ground. Then, in recitativo:)*

                  The wind, sloughing –
                  It must be nothing.

Knights resume the march, singing:

KNIGHTS: We stamp and tramp,
'Til we last encamp
To hoist a trusty flagon –

A tremendous, shrieking roar. A moment of silence, punctuated by a thundering drumbeat.

KNIGHTS: THAT MUST BE THE DRAGON!

Enter the DRAGON.

KNIGHTS: IT *IS* THE DRAGON!

The KNIGHTS, *except* SHAMBLES, *quail before the* DRAGON, *which snorts and roars at the entrance of its lair. The* DRAGON *stamps a clawed paw, and the* KNIGHTS *tremble. They flee offtage, pursued by the* DRAGON, *all exiting stage left, except for* SHAMBLES.

The PRINCESS *and* HANDMAIDEN *emerge from the dark lair, rubbing their eyes. They see* SHAMBLES, *approach.*

PRINCESS: We're grateful, Sir Knight, if this be a rescue—

HANDMAIDEN: But prithee, pray tell, who in th' heck are you?

A forlorn wooden flute and a strummed guitar accompany SIR SHAMBLES *as he takes center stage and sings. Eventually, the* PRINCESS *and* HANDMAIDEN *provide accompaniment.*

THE BALLAD OF SIR SHAMBLES

SHAMBLES: There is a knight
Who rides day and night,
And is known as the good knight, Sir Shambles.
And in any quest
He's the bravest and best,
And many's the road that he rambles.

Like all of the other knights,
He went hunting for mean, ugly dragons to fight.
And, after the dragon he'd smite,
The eggs of the dragon he'd scramble.

It chanced one day
In the knightly way
That Sir Shambles was oft' wont to amble

He came upon
The Very Last Dragon,
And he hid in the thickets and brambles.

The Dragon sang of its sorrowful plight,
And its song touched the heart of our errant knight.
Sir Shambles sat down to consider what's right,
And resolved to be somewhat more humble.

Now, the other knights
Look for dragons to smite,
And they slaughter the dragon that stumbles.

But Sir Shambles thinks
That with dragons extinct,
We'd miss how they make th' Earth rumble.

For dragons aren't such an awful bad lot,
True, they thunder and plunder what men ha'e got—
But without them, romances would have lousy plots,
And let's face it— Most people are numbskulls.

Musical interlude.

There is a knight
Who rides day and night,
And when dragons he finds on his rambles

He bands their legs,
And he hatches their eggs,
And from dragons' paws pulls thorns and brambles.

For dragons now are a species endanger'd,
They're hated, and hunted, fair game for a stranger.
But someone must champion their cause,
            guard their mangers-

The Knight of the Dragons –
Sir Shambles!

The music fades. The PRINCESS *and* HANDMAIDEN *are visibly moved.*

PRINCESS: Wow. I never thought –
                   I never really looked at it that way before.

HANDMAIDEN: He really hasn't hurt us.

PRINCESS: Maybe he just needed somebody to sit on these eggs.

HANDMAIDEN: He *is* kind of cute – When he's sleeping.

PRINCESS: Come on! We may not have a moment to lose!

Hurried exit stage left. Curtain.

Scene iii.   The Beast's Field of Battle.

The Dungeon theme. Enter, from stage right, the KNIGHTS *and the* DRAGON, *battling across the apron of the stage in front of the curtain. Sword blows, slings and arrows, the* DRAGON *roaring and yelping. The* KNIGHTS *get the better of the fight, and the* DRAGON *stumbles to its knees, goes down. The music stops.*

Enter, from stage right, SHAMBLES, *the* PRINCESS, *and* HANDMAIDEN.

The DRAGON *struggles to rise, falls heavily.* SIR ERRANT *raises his sword to slay the* DRAGON, *but* SHAMBLES *draws his own blade and checks* ERRANT's *swing.*

Black.

Scene iv.   The Palace Throne Room

The curtain rises on the Throne Room, the KING *agitated and pacing fitfully. Outside the palace, the* POPULACE *is in open revolt: commotion and chanting outside the windows, the occasional crash of a bottle smashing against the castle walls.* Lords HAL & BURTON *man the cannon at the stage left window, aimed downward into the crowd.*

KING: Shut them up!

HAL & BURTON *light the fuse, put their fingers in their ears and the cannon explodes. The two Lords are knocked on their backsides by the recoil. Silence.*

KING: Much better.

Besieged, the KING *steps downstage, as* HAL & BURTON *move a wide meshed screen in front of him. He addresses the* POPULACE.

THE PLATITUDES

KING:

> I am the Regent of this Land,
> The Admiral of its Seas;
> Defender of the Faith, commanding
> All I oversee.
>
> As Captain of the Ship of State,
> In seas a-storm or swampish –
> I stand this watch, and stand up straight,
> 'Til mission be accomplished.

HAL & BURTON:

> As Captain of the Ship of State,
> In seas a-storm or swampish –
> He stands his watch, and stands up straight,
> And mission is accomplished!

KING:

> The fearsome Dragon shall not pass
> Our flag shall never flag –
> Its colors must hold hard and fast
> And never run nor sag!
>
> Exceptional! Defend we shall!
> For freedom isn't free –

HAL & BURTON:
And the price that must be paid is to
The Hal & Burton Company.

A cabbage is thrown from the pit, hits the screen; then another and another. Tumult, bottles smashing again.

Then the houselights slowly rise as SHAMBLES *leads the* DRAGON *on a rope down the center aisle of the theater. The tumult subsides. The* DRAGON *is porcupined with arrows, limping. The* PRINCESS *and the* HANDMAIDEN *are on either side of the* DRAGON, *assisting it to walk. The bedraggled* KNIGHTS *bring up the rear. The procession halts before the flustered* KING.

KING: What are you waiting for? Knights! Slay the Dragon!

Sirs ERRANT, LESLIE, *and* QUILLIO *listlessly draw their swords.*

PRINCESS: WAIT! DON'T HURT THAT DRAGON.

KING: Why not?

PRINCESS: Because the Dragon never laid a paw on us!

HANDMAIDEN: We were captured, but that Dragon never laid a claw on us!

PRINCESS: He's not that bad a dragon!

HANDMAIDEN: So please, please don't kill him:

Pause.

LESLIE: That's true.

QUILLIO: 'Tis true.

ERRANT: It is.

The KNIGHTS *scabbard their swords. The* KING *appears indecisive.*

HAL & BURTON: Look— Like we told you before—

Piano vamp:

HAL & BURTON: The Dragon Is the Problem of the Kingdom,
                    The root of plague and pestilence and fam—

SHAMBLES: Wait! Cut the music and knock off the song. I've got something to say, and this is important!

The music stops. SHAMBLES *steps in front of the* DRAGON.

SHAMBLES: Look— Admit it— They're right. The Dragon really hasn't done anything all that bad. And dragons will probably become *extinct* if we kill this one. Maybe a living, breathing dragon is better than a *dead* dragon. Maybe we have no right to kill off all the dragons! What about future generations of kids who will never even *see* a dragon? What about all the terrific things that dragons could teach us? And maybe – Just maybe it would be *wrong* to totally kill off one of our fellow creatures!

KING: Maybe, but . . .

KING &
LUCKLESS
PEASANTS   *(After a short pause:)*   NAW!
& HAL
& BURTON:

KING: *(To* Hal & Burton:)

         You two! Make ready to take aim, and fire!

HAL & BURTON *pull the cannon out of the side window, wheel it around to face the* DRAGON. *Not incidentally, the backsides of* HAL & BURTON *are now to the open window.*

KING: Ready!   (HAL *strikes a match.*)
         Aim!   (BURTON *aims the cannon.*)

SIR SHAMBLES, *interposing himself between the* DRAGON *and the cannon, raises his shield. The* PRINCESS, *and then the* HANDMAIDEN, *break away from the* DRAGON *and stand with* SHAMBLES.

PRINCESS: WAIT!

Have pity, father.
Show mercy, my King!
Stay thy hand from slaughter –
Let him live to sing!

HAL'*s match goes out.*

PRINCESS' ARIA

I
Never thought that I'd
Ever take the side
Of a thing so thunder-full

But I
See something in its eye
Old as earth and sky –
An understanding wonderful.

How could I have neither seen nor heard
But somehow always known;
What, awakened to a wider world,
I'm touched and told and shown.

So my
Heart shall ere abide
Always at the side
Of this beast so blunder-full

For I
Know deep down inside
Under that hard hide
Another heart as vulner'ble.

And since now must be the time of man,
To man I must avow:
That this is something magical
Entrusted to us now.

Have pity, father.
Show mercy, my King!
Stay thy hand from slaughter –
Let him live to sing!

Awestruck silence.

KING: FIRE! *(Pause.)* Hal & Burton – FIRE THAT GUN!

HAL *strikes a match and torches the fuse as* BURTON *aims the cannon at the* DRAGON. *The* KING *frantically gesticulates for them to hurry.* HAL & BURTON, *their backs to the open window, put their fingers in their ears. The cannon explodes and the recoil knocks* HAL & BURTON *backwards and through the open window, defenestrating them. Exeunt the Royal Ministers* LORDS HAL & BURTON.

Pause.

SHAMBLES, *the* PRINCESS, *and the* HANDMAIDEN *turn to look at the* DRAGON, *which is unharmed. Then the* KING *sinks to his knees and a bowling ball rolls out from under his cloak.*

PRINCESS: *(In disbelief:)* He called to 'fire.'

HANDMAIDEN: *(Approaching to comfort her:)* Yes.

PRINCESS: . . . And so was struck down, upon his own command.

HANDMAIDEN: By his own hand. *(Pause.)* But more truly, by his mouth – that made the order stand. *(Pause, frustrated.)* Must we still rhyme everything?

PRINCESS: Is – dead the King?

SHAMBLES: *(Kneeling at the fallen* KING) The King, Princess, is dead.

HANDMAIDEN: And you are Queen.

PRINCESS: . . . I thought I should feel something .

SHAMBLES: *(Having approached the* QUEEN:) You *don't?*

Faint and solemn musical Underscore:

PRINCESS: How am I to make, sudden, this thing sensible?
                 That dulls the senses like a dream, dissembling –
                 Yet bids me speak, as critics would, in trembling
                 At such dramatic turn, sharp and improbable.

                 A Queen must, from the first, be honest
                 Or else alights upon her, th' single filament
                 That cobwebs into lies, and un-truths consequent;
                 Ensnaring, 'til our problems are beyond us.

                 And so, first it must be said, that I feel nothing
                 An' th' glands and loins and limbs that did beget me
                 Can no more pull a bowstring taut, arrow'd, to prick; –

                 And Caesars, kaisers, czars, tycoons, and kings
                 That postured and pronounced, dead and impotent be
                 To decry that th' Crown, this hour crown'd –
                 Decrees a picnic.

QUILLIO: The King is dead!

LESLIE: Long live the Queen!

The fawning CHORUS, *again, anthemic:*

HARK & HAIL

CHORUS:

Hark & hail our high and mighty
Chief Executive Officer!
Tho' dark the gale and nigh the lightning
Sail on ship of state
Evermore!

Tho' the maw of death ope' wide ahead
Ever onward! Stay the course!

QUEEN: *(Self-possessed:)* Enough!

The CHORUS, *cued, quiets.* ERRANT *approaches the* QUEEN, *kneels.*

ERRANT: The late King, my fair Queen, decreed
To all in this brave Land:
That he who delivers the Dragon's ears
Should win his daughter's hand!

QUEEN: And so the first rule of this new crown'd Realm
I do announce, repealing all
Former and contrary Promulgations,
Laws, Commands, Proscriptions, Dictums, Canons,
Doctrines, Dogma, Protocols, Pronouncements,
Maxims, Axioms, Codes, Precepts, and Ordinances:

The Dragon's life is hereby – spared!

The DRAGON *looks quizzically about as he is surrounded by the cheering assemblage.*

QUEEN: Our second rule, quite like the first,
                     Repeals a Quirk and capricious Whim
                     Of our late Sovereign:

                     We shall have no more – unnecessary – rhyming!

ALL *cheer, and exeunt, in procession.*

CURTAIN.

The CURTAIN CALL is a full cast reprise of THE VERY LAST DRAGON, *the final bow taken by the two people who have played the* DRAGON, *fore and aft, now separated and respectively costumed.*

FINAL CURTAIN.

Cradlesong

There's grass for the cattle
And feed for the sheep,
There's hay for the horses
And corn for the geese;
And the fishes eat fishes
In the millpond so deep

In the kitchen, the cradle
Is rocking empty.

In the straw, in the stable,
The hound, half asleep
Gives suck to the puppies
She cossets and keeps;
And high in the rafters
The barnswallows sweep

In the kitchen, the cradle
Is rocking gently.

The mare is unsaddled
And dreaming, she leaps
In a meadow of clover
With no bit in her teeth;
And the stallion is grazing
On the hillside so steep

In the kitchen, the cradle
Is rocking empty.

Morning of the Armistice

On the morning of the armistice
no fuses hissed
the poisoned mist was lifted.
No broken roof or rifle fire
fell upon deaf ears,
no tongue resisted.

The trumpets called, the snare drums rolled,
the churchbells tolled from steeples
for an hour.
And down below the windowsill
the streets were filled with people
throwing flowers.

Regiments of soldiers
broke their swords and swore to nevermore
raise up the fighting cry;
They followed, bearing flags of black
a man on horseback
riding high.

The Death of Rumpelstiltskin

Notes for a Law Lecture
by Russell Fox

Translation of the Tale by Lucy Crane
Illustrations by Walter Crane, *at al.*

ANCIENT LIGHTS BOOKS

The Death of Rumpelstiltskin

Notes for a Law Lecture

Written 2009-2012
Buffalo, New York

Ancient Lights Books Octavo Edition Series #2
First Printing 2012

Translation by Lucy Crane
and illustrations by Walter Crane, H.J. Ford,
John B. Gruelle and George Cruickshank
are in the Public Domain.

With thanks to my father,
and to my stepchildren & children.

Ancient Lights Books
www.ancientlightsbooks.com

Great is Justice;
Justice is not settled by legislatures and laws . . . . it is in the soul,
It cannot be varied by statutes any more than love or pride or the
    attraction of gravity can,

It is immutable . . . . it does not depend on majorities . . . . majorities or
    what not come at last before the same passionless and exact tribunal.

— Walt Whitman
From *Great are the Myths*
LEAVES OF GRASS, 1855 ED.

Jacob & Wilhelm Grimm, by Hermann Grimm

Acknowledgment

Dortchen and Lisette Wild, sisters, probably first told the story of *Rumpelstilzchen* to the brothers Jacob and Wilhelm Grimm in 1808, the year after Napoleon's armies occupied the Kingdom of Hesse. The Wild and Grimm households were across the street from each other in the Hessian city of Kassel, which had come under the rule of Napoleon's incompetent brother, Jérôme Bonaparte, whom Napoleon had installed on the throne of the redrawn Kingdom of Westphalia. The Kingdom of Hesse was thereby abolished – like the other defeated kingdoms and fiefdoms and free cities of the Holy Roman Empire, which the French had overrun. Jacob and Wilhelm Grimm, in their early twenties and both former law students at the University of Marburg, were now idled scholars.

Living under the French occupation like that, the Grimms became politicized. Both of them spoke French, but neither wanted anything to do with living as subjects in a vassal state of the Napoleonic Empire. Instead, they dreamed of a day when all the former dominions of the conquered Holy Roman Empire would come together in a new nation of the German speaking peoples, once the French were out. It would be the nation that it always should have been, the people of its some two hundred kingdoms and principalities united into one country by their common language and literature and culture, high and low. A heritage. The Grimms, being philologists, looked to the kind of story traditionally told by the peasantry to their children – the folk tale – and saw in these stories the cradle of the Deutschland nation.

So while they were under the French occupation, the brothers Grimm turned to gathering the stories for their collection of the folk tales of the German speaking peoples, KINDER-UND- HAUSMÄRCHEN (*Children's and Household Tales*). As the legend would have it, some of the tales were indeed recorded on the Grimms' trips into the countryside, collected from old peasant women. Others were researched in university libraries, where the Grimms found suitably *volkish* stories and copied them out of old books and manuscripts. But most of the tales were told to the Grimms by middle-class schoolgirls like the Wild sisters.

The first volume of KINDER-UND-HAUSMÄRCHEN — eighty-six stories including *Rotkäppchen (Little Red Riding Hood)*, *Sneewittchen (Snow White)*, *Rapunzel*, and *Rumpelstilzchen* — was published in 1812, the year before Napoleon's armies retreated across Europe and withdrew from the city of Kassel. A second volume of seventy more stories appeared in 1815, and six more editions followed. Wilhelm Grimm published a selection of the fifty tales deemed most suitable for children in 1825, the same year that he and Dortchen Wild were married after a long engagement. Wilhelm and Dortchen would have three children; Jacob Grimm never married.

In his earliest incarnation, Rumpelstilzchen came to a different end: he simply "ran away angrily, and never came back." It was probably Wilhelm Grimm who revised the story for later editions of KINDER-UND-HAUSMÄRCHEN, until the 1857 version, in which the little man accomplishes his *denouement* in a manner that is quite more spectacular, and memorable.

Lucy Crane's was one of many nineteenth century translations of *Rumpelstilzchen* into *Rumpelstiltskin*. She worked from the definitive 1857 edition of KINDER-UND-HAUSMÄRCHEN, rendering 52 of the Grimms' tales into English to provide the text for a book that was "done into pictures" by her younger brother, Walter Crane. Their collaboration, entitled HOUSEHOLD STORIES FROM THE COLLECTION OF THE BROS. GRIMM, was designed by the Macmillan company to capitalize on Walter Crane's popularity as a children's book illustrator: in the first edition, the table of contents listed his pictures, but was without any reference to the titles of the stories. Later printings remedied this, but *Illustrated by Walter Crane* was usually the only cover credit, and Miss Crane's translation was generally overlooked.

HOUSEHOLD STORIES FROM THE COLLECTION OF THE BROS. GRIMM first appeared in England in 1882, the year of Lucy Crane's death, at age forty. The book was reprinted in America a year later.

Walter Crane would live for another thirty-three years, until 1915. In that time he became an established member of the European arts and crafts school, designing *art nouveau* textiles and wallpaper, stained glass, and Wedgewood china. He also became a Socialist, and drew cartoons for Socialist magazines and newspapers. He lectured on art and design, and museums exhibited his easel paintings. His great professional disappointment, however, was that he achieved widespread fame only for his illustration of children's books; at the end of his life, he reportedly felt that his work as a serious artist had been unjustly disregarded. By then, Lucy Crane's accomplishment as a translator was largely forgotten.[1] Even today, the work of the illustrator Walter Crane gets a three page entry in The Norton Anthology of Children's Literature, which footnotes his sister's literary contribution to his books only once in passing, and mentions their sibling collaboration on HOUSEHOLD STORIES not at all.[2]

But while Walter Crane's illustrations are available today only in a paperback reprint, Lucy Crane's translation of *Rumpelstiltskin* has become the version of the story that most often appears in fairy tale collections and anthologies of children's literature, sometimes accompanied by the work of contemporary illustrators, and usually without crediting Miss Crane. This has been true for the better part of century, and persists: Borders' 2007 selection of the Grimms' tales and Barnes and Noble's gilt edged, gold embossed, deluxe 2008 edition both   use Lucy Crane's translation of *Rumpelstiltskin* in the now standard fashion; *i.e.*, without attribution. So, although it was first published more than a century and a quarter ago, and other translations have come and gone and are re-made anew every few years, Lucy Crane's *Rumpelstiltskin* is still the rendition that most children are likely to know, if they are familiar with the story at all.

---

[1]   Also forgotten is Lucy Crane's early role in the Arts and Crafts movement, advancing the aesthetic that the "the common things of life" should be both practical and beautiful. *See,* Crane, Lucy, ART AND THE FORMATION OF TASTE: SIX LECTURES (Chautauqua Press, Boston, 1885), published posthumously. Charles Goodrich Whiting's preface to these "unpretentious lectures" gives us the only description of (by then, the deceased) Lucy Crane that we are likely to get: "The lovely nature, both sweet and strong, of their author, informs her gracious and intelligent instruction with a fine charm; and she leads her disciples, by a hand as firm as it is gentle, to the safe and true ground of taste and judgment." A ghost hand, already then, and countenance.

[2]   Zipes, et al., eds, 2005, pp. 399-401.

There is good reason for this, beyond the practical fact that Lucy Crane's work has passed into the public domain, and so is no longer protected by copyright. Miss Crane's translations of the Grimms' stories are spare, compelling, enchanting and haunting. Her retelling of the tales of the Brothers Grimm is, quite appropriately, magical.

So acknowledgment is hereby made for the extensive use herein of Lucy Crane's translation of *Rumpelstiltskin,* a German fairy tale collected by the brothers Jacob and Wilhelm Grimm during the Napoleonic occupation, when their beloved Kassel was a captive city in the Kingdom of Westphalia — which, translated from the French, means *the best of all possible worlds.*

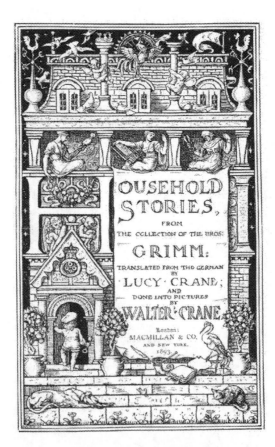

Part 1

Miller's Daughter

There once was a miller who was poor, but he had one beautiful daughter.

So begins the story of Rumpelstiltskin, with a *miller* who *once was*, and who *was poor*.

That is the first thing we are told, and so it must be important. It tells us one of two things about the miller: either that he *is no more*, or that he *is no longer poor*, by the time this story is being told. We are not told which.

With such a beginning, we are led to expect that this may be a tale about the miller. And because we are told for a fact that the miller was *poor*, we might also expect the story to follow a standard fairy tale plot: will the miller get rich, or not, and how? There are many such tales in the Grimms' canon, in which a poor but aspiring protagonist sets out into the world, and encounters a magical helper and faces fantastic tests, and thereby either wins his fortune or foolishly loses it.

But those stories are never about millers. They instead tend to be about youngest sons, denied property and inheritance under the feudal rule of primogeniture; or roaming soldiers, summarily discharged and left pfennigless after the wars. There are also tales about apprentices escaped from harsh masters, and mistreated stepchildren, and forsaken daughters. And surprisingly many of the Grimms' stories concern impoverished tailors, who were typically without any fair prospect of making a living at the low-skilled trade of tailoring. Such protagonists can be clever or dense, kind or selfish, lucky or not, but what they have in common is that they have nothing to lose, and so venture abroad into an unknown and enchanted world.

A miller, on the other hand, was unlikely to strike out on the wide open road in search of his fortune. He had a trade, was bound to the mill ground. He either owned the mill or tended it. He might be poor, but because his livelihood was grinding flour, he would never go hungry, and so he would never go out wandering. He was neither a peasant, landless and destitute, nor a discontented prince, who might go a-roving in search of a bride.

64

Rather, the millers in the KINDER-UND-HAUSMÄRCHEN are an unadventurous lot, and worse. Too accustomed to the dulling rote of the grindstone, they are afflicted by "habitual and uncreative thinking" and have been said to symbolize greed. (Olderr 1986). Examples abound. In one story, appropriately entitled *The Maiden without Hands* (KHM 31), an ignorant miller barters his beautiful and pious daughter to the devil, and later cravenly does the devil's bidding by cutting off her hands. In another, *The Robber Bridegroom* (KHM 40), a miller blithely marries off his beautiful daughter to a mysterious stranger who, yes, turns out to be a robber bridegroom. *The Devil with the Three Golden Hairs* (KHM 29) features a miller and his wife who obediently allow an evil king to dispatch their foundling child with a sealed letter to his queen, which commands that the child is to be immediately killed and buried. And in *The Nixie in the Pond* (KHM 181), a poor miller bargains with a water witch, who thereby claims possession of his newborn son.

Accordingly, a miller in the Grimm's tales may be a coward or a cuckold or a fool, but he is also, almost invariably, a *bad parent*.

So a miller is never the hero in the Grimms' tales, and *Rumpelstilzchen* is not about the miller. Neither will it truly be about Rumpelstiltskin. Instead it will be about the miller's *one beautiful daughter*. She is immediately eligible to be the protagonist of the tale, inasmuch as she is *beautiful*. But, curiously, her beauty will never be mentioned again in the tale, nor will it help her.

She may not have been his only daughter – the poor miller may have been burdened by other daughters, ugly or plain – but she is his *one beautiful daughter*, and the only reason the miller is at all notable.

And, typically for a miller, he will carelessly put this one beautiful daughter at great risk, and for next to nothing.

It happened one day that he came to speak
with the king, and to give himself consequence,
he told him that he had a daughter
who could spin gold out of straw.

The king said to the miller,
"That is an art that pleases me well;
if thy daughter is as clever as you say,
bring her to my castle tomorrow,
that I may put her to the proof."

Now, keep in mind that the people who are almost always being told this tale are *children*. And some of them are little girls, who are likely to swiftly identify with the miller's *one beautiful daughter*. If you are a little girl listening to the story, you are already paying close attention to the circumstances of miller's daughter, and probably feel sorry for her. The miller, her father, is a poor provider. And now the miller introduces himself to *the king*, with the reckless boast that he is a person of consequence because his daughter *can spin gold out of straw*.

This is positively frightening, for every little girl knows that she herself cannot spin gold out of straw, and could never. And even if little girls nowadays do not quite know what *spinning* is, they know that the miller could not be *poor* if his daughter could truly *spin gold out of straw*. So the miller cannot be telling the truth to the king. And children know, too, that a *king* is always a person of truly great consequence and power, and that the miller's false claim of his daughter's magical abilities to such an exalted personage may very well put her in real danger.

Because even children know about *kings*. But most adults have either forgotten, or never learned in school, that there was once a time when there really *were* kings, and many of them. Kings are now the stuff of fairy tales, but the Grimms were born at a time, and in a part of the world, when a mere locality was apt to have its own sovereign regent, with all the royal prerogatives and regalia attendant thereto.

For more than a thousand years, since the coronation of the emperor Charlemagne on Christmas day in 800 A.D., the German speaking peoples had lived in a fragmented territory of some three hundred separate and sovereign principalities — kingdoms and dukedoms and fiefdoms, bishoprics and archbishoprics, margraves and free cities — which would come to be called the Holy Roman Empire. It was more a conglomeration of medieval dominions and freeholds than an actual empire, and it was Roman only insofar as its titular emperors were crowned by the Roman Catholic popes. After Martin Luther, in about 1500, it would no longer even be uniformly Roman Catholic. From then on, the religion of each principality was a matter to be decided by its particular sovereign, along with everything else of consequence.

In a patchwork empire where all the important politics was truly local, culture, too, was parochial. Artists and composers were beholden to the patronage of petty monarchs or the caprices of rich archbishops, resulting in a lot of marches and masses. Mozart, incapable of such obsequy, has a strong claim to being the first modern artist: it was a courageous thing for Mozart to break out of his sinecure as a church music composer for the archbishopric of Salzburg, in 1791, with the untried idea that he might make a living on private commissions for his secular compositions, and by giving subscription concerts. He failed in financial terms, as great artists sometimes do, but Mozart's personal rebellion against the system of court patronage was a revolutionary act, some twenty years before Napoleon Bonaparte would finally deal the death blow to the Holy Roman Empire.

By then, Beethoven was celebrating Napoleon as the liberator of Europe, initially titling the first draft of his Third Symphony *Bonaparte* in homage to the First Consul of France. But when Napoleon proclaimed himself emperor, and thereby betrayed the ideals of the Enlightenment, Beethoven famously changed the dedication "to the memory of a great man." In 1812, when the Grimms first published *Rumpelstilzchen*, Napoleon Bonaparte was still the conqueror of Central Europe, and parents were keeping their children in line with scary stories of *Old Bony*.

THE DEATH OF RUMPELSTILTSKIN

There was a tradition for this, going back well before Napoleon. There were good kings and bad kings; wise and generous sovereigns, and tyrants who were both capricious and cruel. In such a world, the character of a prince was important. A girl might thrill to a tale of a virtuous maid being wed to a good prince (often met while out wandering his kingdom *incognito*), but the fate of being married off to an evil king was frightening.

A little boy, having heard only this much of *Rumpelstilzchen*, might be impatient for something more happen. There is nobody, yet, to identify with. A little girl is more likely to wait with a feeling of impending dread, knowing full well that the miller's daughter has an idiot for a father, to make such a ridiculous claim to a *king*, and all *to give himself consequence*. Puffery. And the king calls the miller's bluff, but of course it will not be the miller who will be put to the test. The king decrees that the miller must deliver up his daughter, who must face a trial in which only her cleverness can save her.

We have, then, the first of the wildly asymmetrical exchanges that will structure the plot of *Rumpelstilzchen*. In exchange for a fleeting moment of self-important preening before his king, on a whim, the miller trades all he has, his one beautiful daughter, *to give himself consequence.* It is for this that the miller makes his brief appearance at the beginning of the story, sets the tale in motion, and then is not heard from or told about again. So the Miller is a minor character, a small man.

But fortunately, the protagonist children of the Grimm's tales are almost always able to transcend bad parenting, which is interesting. It's a consistent theme, an optimistic take on the youth of the coming generation, whom the Brothers Grimm were betting on to people their new nation. So our attention now turns to the miller's daughter, and to how she will meet her test.

When the girl was brought to him,
he led her into a room that was quite full of straw,
and gave her a wheel and spindle, and said,

"Now set to work, and if by the early morning
thou hast not spun this straw into gold
thou shalt die."

And he shut the door himself,
and left her there alone.

The poor girl. Our hearts go out to her. She is there for no fault of her own, locked in a stone castle room that has been pitched full of stable straw, probably at sundown, and told by the king himself that if by dawn she has not spun it all into gold, she shall die.

It is *not her fault*. It is *unfair*.

And that is the premise of a good many of the Grimms' stories: that life can turn suddenly and shockingly unfair, often to a mere youth, who must then set about the quest of confronting and outwitting such injustice. The tales are full of such youths — mere children put out in the woods, youngest sons cut off without inheritance, mistreated apprentices, cashiered soldiers.

But the miller's daughter does not look like this kind of typical Grimm's protagonist. She seems helpless, has said nothing in protest to the king, even when so cruelly put to such an absurdly impossible task. The very arbitrariness of the contest takes her breath away, leaves her speechless. She is unprepared and ill-equipped, neither lucky nor tricky, without the help of an older and wiser sibling, or the boundless optimism of a bootless son, or the clever tongue of an escaped apprentice, or the seasoned wit of some brigand soldier. She is not — at least, not yet — a trickster. And she did not, like many of the Grimms' heroes, decide (against advice or common wisdom) to strike out on her own into the great wide world, ready to take up any challenge that might happen along, to fight or outfox any adversary or circumstance, and thereby find her fortune. This business of spinning gold out of straw was not her idea.

Nor has the tale at its outset afforded the miller's daughter with any opportunity, as so often presented in the Grimms' tales, to demonstrate her deserving virtue. The story does not show her journey on the road to the palace, where she might have charitably assisted an old crone with her burden of tinder sticks at the wayside, or done something so simple as free a bird from a snare. We do not know whether she set out on the journey dutifully alone, or was followed or led all the way by her father, or what resolve she might have shown upon her approach to the gates of the castle.

Instead, the miller's daughter makes an abrupt appearance and is immediately ushered into a castle room, heaped to the ceiling with straw, where she is suddenly confronted with the insoluble riddle of turning, spinning, straw into gold. And she is put under the threat of death if she cannot do it, which is *doubly* unfair.[3]

Since this is a tale about transactions, it could be said that the miller's daughter must give the king a room full of spun gold, in exchange for her life. But, significantly, this is not proposed by the king as an offer, a bartered-for transaction, a contractual bargain. It is an ultimatum. The king is the supreme authority, absolute, unchallengeable. And the king, ominously, has taken a personal interest in the matter. It is the king, himself, who cruelly shuts the door, and leaves her there in that straw-filled room, alone.

---

[3]   The prospect of one's *own* death being, always, *singularly* unfair.

And so the poor miller's daughter
was left there sitting,
and could not think what to do for her life:

she had no notion how to set to work to spin gold
from straw, and her distress grew so great
that she began to weep.

The tale pauses for a simple picture: a vignette of the miller's daughter, poor and without influence or means, unable to think her way out of the predicament of her impending death. Any cleverness fails her now; she is utterly powerless, without knowledge. She has no idea about how she could even begin to accomplish such an incomprehensible thing as spinning gold from straw. It is a challenge even beyond the Arthurian feat of pulling the sword from the stone. *That*, at least, would be an achievement of human ingenuity: of the smelting of ore and the tempering of steel and the hammering of the white-hot metal into the shape and sharpness of a blade.

To turn straw into gold, on the other hand, was *alchemy*. The great preoccupation of occultist chemists since Hellenistic Egypt, and after that the futile pursuit of Faustian doctors in medieval times, *alchemy* was the attempt to transmute lesser substances, usually base metals, into gold. A grail. In the Mediterranean, and later northwards, the cellars and attics of the great timber-and-stone universities of Europe were habited by a faculty that fired and mixed powdered elements, boiled and smelted metals (especially lead, probably because it, too, was a heavy metal), and distilled and re-distilled the hot liquefaction of purified ores together with concoctions of arcane ingredients, herbs and oils and blood, all in the quest to alchemize gold.

And all to naught. But, in retrospect, alchemy is today regarded as a *proto-science* — perhaps *the* proto-science — inasmuch as the vaunted side-achievement of all those cold centuries of calibrated trial and inevitable error would come to be esteemed as *the scientific method* — the systematized solving of recognized conundrums by hypothesis and experimentation — a carefully prescribed approach that would eventually claim to illumine the movement of the heavens, explain the creation of the earth, and posit the evolution of its creatures, though never producing any gold.

Indeed, by the time of the rendering of *Rumpelstilzche*[4] alchemy had already been discredited, even among the peasantry, as a fraudulent scheme of charlatans, the hawking of mountebanks. But *gold* was still important, paradoxically because nobody had discovered how to transmute it from lead, or anything else.

And so, during this pause, a digression: concerning the medium of exchange in this tale that is so much about transactions, which is *gold.*

What is it about *gold* that makes it the stuff of so many myths and tales and entertainments, the device and excuse for so many plots, from Midas to the Sierra Madre? In *The Wealth of Nations,* serendipitously published in 1776, Adam Smith explained the allure and value of gold and silver as arising "partly from their utility, and partly from their beauty." But far more important, in an economy of grasping prehensiles, is the fact of the comparative rarity of silver and gold. "The actual price, however, seems not to be necessarily determined by any thing but the actual scarcity or plenty of these metals themselves." Small supply, big demand.

And if their scarcity is what makes certain metals valuable, it is also what for so long made them a dependable medium of exchange, a logical coinage. Adam Smith, in 1776, again:

> This value was antecedent to and independent of their being used as coins, and was the quality which fitted them for that employment. That employment, however, by occasioning a new demand, and by diminishing the quantity which could be employed in any other way, may have afterwards contributed to keep up or increase their value.

---

[4]   Unintended pun, left in.

The critical insight, here, is about *money*, which Adam Smith suggested need not be coined from precious metals. A radical idea in 1776, more than half a century after Sir Isaac Newton (as Chancellor of the Exchequer) had effectively wedded Great Britain to the gold standard, and after that for much of the now forgotten history of the United States, which was greatly concerned with the fiercely partisan issue of divorcing the dollar from gold.[5] Both Great Britain and the United States would suspend the convertibility of gold into notes during periods of grave national crises, the Napoleonic and Civil Wars respectively,[6] but both nations would return to gold as the standard of fixed currency when those wars were over. And this gold-based monetary policy, though now an aside in the survey-course history textbooks, was the great economic issue of the age.

This is because the fundamental problem with tying a currency to gold is that such "hard" money, redeemable in gold, is *tight* money. It has been said that all the gold ever mined would fit into an Olympic-sized swimming pool.[7] Whether or not this is factually accurate, there has certainly never been enough gold to go around, at least in a democracy subject to the demands of popular suffrage. William Jennings Bryant would valiantly campaign against this "Cross of Gold" as a three-time Democrat nominee for president, and would be a three-time loser. American currency would remain pegged to the price of gold[8] until Richard Nixon, in 1971, repudiated the post-war Bretton Woods Agreements.

---

[5]   In the American presidential election of 1892, for example, James Baird Weaver won several western states (Kansas, Colorado, Nevada, Idaho) on the People's Party (or Populist, formerly Greenback) ticket, advocating the frankly inflationary policy that the gold standard should be abandoned and that money be coined in the more abundant (and domestically mined) precious metal of silver. The Populist Party's electoral success has pretty much been omitted from the textbooks, probably because Weaver was a dangerous anti-corporation radical, with arguments and invective that are incisively damning, even by contemporary standards. *See* Weaver, James B., *A Call to Action* (1892).

[6]   Great Britain would temporarily go off the gold standard during the Napoleonic wars, when the Brothers Grimm were busy collecting the tales of KINDER-UND-HAUSMÄRCHEN. Lincoln would put the U.S.A. on paper currency (while the C.S.A. had something like a cotton-backed currency, which famously busted) during the Civil War.

[7]   Okay — full disclosure, here: per the internet, and so possibly suspect. Doesn't *sound* right.

[8]   At approx. $35 per ounce.

What was left after Nixon was *paper* currency, backed by the full faith and credit of the United States, but intrinsically worthless in the view of the proponents of the School of Austrian Economists, such as Ludwig von Mises, and the popular polemicist Ayn Rand.[9] Rand peopled her most weighty novel with a cast of industrial titans who go underground and mint gold and silver coins to trade amongst themselves, refusing to accept any currency that is not based upon "*objective* values."[10] Whatever this may exactly mean, it is squarely in the tradition of regarding precious metals as the only legitimate form of currency — a supposition that persists unto our own time.[11]

But, in fact, any commodity that is of limited (or limitable) supply may pragmatically work as a medium of exchange. Thus, across a whole swath of forgotten history, cowry seashells (being, then and there, rare) served as the currency for Muslim traders operating out of the Middle East. And consumables, unconsumed, have always been ready money in times and places of scarcity: hence, cigarettes have famously been the medium of exchange in concentration camps and black markets; and, today, copper pipes stripped from vacant properties, and cocaine in inch-square self-sealable plastic packets, and products so cumbersome as jugs of laundry detergent are readily bartered, at generally fixed values; all as fungible as the more precious metals. The very word *salary* is derived from the Latin *salt*, the commodity in which the Roman

---

[9]   Nixon had to do this, incidentally, because the French, under Charles de Gaulle, were trading in their dollar reserves for U.S. government gold, thereby deliberately undermining the U.S. dollar. A scant quarter century before, it should be recalled, America had rescued France from Nazi occupation, and had charitably put General de Gaulle right up at the front of the big military parade that marched into the liberated Paris. No good deed, alas, goes unpunished.

[10]   *ATLAS SHRUGGED,* © Ayn Rand, 1957 (Centennial Edition, 2005), p. 727. Of her heroine, the only female industrial titan in the book, upon being hired as a maid and offered an advance, Rand memorably wrote this:

She was startled to discover, as her hand reached for the gold piece, that she felt the eager, desperate, tremulous hope of a young girl on her first job: the hope that she would be able to deserve it.

"Yes, sir," she said, her eyes lowered. (p. 761)

[11]   At this writing, the Libertarian Ron Paul has continued the quaint American tradition of basing a quixotic presidential campaign on the issue of monetary policy; in this most recent iteration, advocating a return to the gold standard and the abolition of the Federal Reserve System.

legionnaires were paid.   And, although not a consumable, even U.S. government issued paper currency, so long as its supply is sufficiently restricted, is still as good as gold, and can buy it. The fact that some ninety-seven percent of a scheming American citizenry has so far been unable to earn and accrue and accumulate so much as a single million dollars in such paper money is, I submit, conclusive proof that the United States' supply of printed currency is being quite effectively managed by the powers that be — the Federal Reserve System — for the most part. We might not like it, but there it is. And it works, at least for now.

So Ludwig von Mises and Ayn Rand and Ron Paul look like they are fundamentally wrong about economics. There is nothing intrinsically magical, after all, about gold.

That said, gold is still gold. It has been the McGuffin[12] of most tales, from Jason's quest for the golden fleece to every trove of bullion in the bank vaults of modern heist thrillers. And it does, at this point in the story, seem to be the McGuffin of *Rumpelstiltskin*, as well —   precisely because we know that *gold* cannot be spun out of something so plenteous, and thus so worthless, as *straw*.

The miller's daughter knows this, too. And so she is mystified, clueless, terrified. She weeps with of the grief of the condemned, sitting at the idle spinning wheel and overwhelmed by the straw heaped high all around her. She is a poor and pitiable figure, and we have so far been given no reason to believe in her, cast our lot with her.

Except for the fact that she is beautiful.

---

[12]   A *McGuffin*, per the pioneering movie director Alfred Hitchcock, is an object that is *perceived* as being of great value, such that it suffices to drive the plot, provides the scenario for the dialogue, makes for narrative. Hence the falcon statuette in Hitchcock's *The Maltese Falcon*, reputed to be a precious Egyptian artifact, is ultimately but a counterfeit: a plaster cast, painted black. Only when Bogart busts it open and spills out the diamonds hidden inside are we shocked into the recognition that the actual statuette, the Maltese *McGuffin*, has been a mere excuse for a plot, the physical thing of it worthless all along, as discardable as a cardboard box: packaging. But it doesn't matter. None of it. We see that even had there never been any diamonds cached inside the fake plaster bird, all this has been to push a plotline: what people will do to get what they believe can buy their freedom. It never does, of course, but that is the Moral of such Tales. *Rumpelstiltskin*, we will see, is not one of them.

We have been told only that about her. That she is the miller's *one beautiful daughter.* And so we picture her in helpless despair at the unspinning wheel, its pedal idle and the spindle empty; the miller's daughter sitting probably in the straw on the floor, downcast and beautiful with her head bent and her golden hair hanging. The vignette could be one of those picturesque black cast-iron statues in a typical German town square: like the donkey, dog, cat and rooster, in Bremen; or the fairy-tale statue of the goose boy, with a fat bird under each arm, in old Nuremberg. *Miller's Daughter, at idle Loom.*

Illustration by H.J. Ford

Then all at once the door opened,
and in came a little man, who said

"Good evening, miller's daughter;
why are you crying?"
"Oh," answered the girl,
"I have got to spin gold out of straw,
and don't understand the business."

We have here — in this next single sentence — the abrupt & dramatic & magical entrance of the (ultimately) titular character of this tale — *Rumpelstiltskin* — although as to the *little man*, who so courteously greets the *miller's daughter*, we have not yet in the narrative been outrightly given his name. But even a half-clever child, told beforehand the title of the story, has probably already guessed it.

This puts the child one step ahead of *the girl*, who in the very next sentence demonstrates that she is not only wholly ignorant of the business of spinning gold from straw, but also that she is so socially inept that she does not think to pause for the customary nicety of introducing herself. She neither offers the little man her own name nor asks him his, a discourtesy. This will play, later.

But neither does she even think to inquire as to how the little man might already know her to be the daughter of a miller. Rather, she blurts out her problem in her instant first words — *"I have got to spin gold out of straw, and don't understand the business."* Granted, the problem of having to spin gold from straw is daunting, and especially with the penalty of death looming at dawn if she cannot accomplish it, but the miller's daughter is both impolite and incurious, abrupt and self-absorbed, obdurate. These are hardly endearing traits, even when considered by little girls who, while closely listening to the story, have been (so far) predisposed to empathize with a poor and beautiful miller's daughter. So, despite her understandable panic at being put in so immediate a plight, whether the miller's daughter will indeed be the heroine of the tale is called into question by the very first words that she speaks in it; neither asking the identity of her visitor, nor how he knows who she is.[13]

The little *boys* hearing the tale, on the other hand, have finally been given somebody to root for. Typically oblivious to female beauty, the immature male listenership of the tale has likely not bought into the idea of the miller's daughter as either interesting or sympathetic, does not *identify* with her. Rumpelstiltskin, on the other hand, is a different kind of character altogether. And what *he* is, so self-evidently, is a *little man* – somebody their own size, who is pretty cool, magically appearing & capably knowledgeable & already taking command of the situation, a potential rescuer. Little boys look for heroes, not heroines. And from the moment the door all at once opens and in comes Rumpelstiltskin, he is mysterious and magically powerful, and fascinates.

Good parents, of course, are more cautious. Rumpelstiltskin is a stranger. And not only a stranger, but strange. A *little man*. In the German original, *ein kleines Männchen*. And although not the German word for dwarf – *zwerc* – there is nonetheless immediately something about him that recalls the *volkish* archetype of the dwarf Alberich, chieftain of the Nibelungen and hoarder of the Rheingold, venal and intriguing and wicked.[14] Both little men are outsiders, underworld characters, who labor in the glow of gold. Unpredictable and dangerous to have dealings, with diminutive tricksters. Adults somehow suspect this about Rumpelstiltskin, upon the moment of his inexplicable entrance, without being able to explain quite why.

---

[13]   A possible alternative explanation: maybe she takes it for granted that her plight is known throughout the palace – that everybody who is anybody has already heard the backstairs gossip about the poor girl who has been so tragically shut up in a room full of straw and tasked with spinning it all into gold, upon pain of death – and that everybody knows that this unlucky girl is the unfortunate daughter of a foolishly boastful miller. But the girl does not ask about that, or for his name, or anything. She is impolite, myopic, self-ish. The little man thus skips the introductions and gets right down to business. He offers his help, but in the form of a proposal, inviting a transaction. *What will you give me, if – ?*

[14]   And, according to Theodor Adorno, and many various others, the negative stereotype of a *Jew*. More on this later, in the second half of this *klein buch. See,* WIKIPEDIA, *Alberich,* circa 2012.

But we should not forget that the little man comes in when she is weeping, abject & desperate & in tears; and that he does, after properly greeting her, ask her why it is that she is crying. The door that the king has so emphatically shut, perhaps locked, has magically swept open on its hinges, and the little man is manifestly there to solve all her problems, which are lethally serious, when nobody else will be coming to help her. And she is truly in need of somebody's help, awaits any champion, is facing death. The king isn't joking, even if he regards the miller's boast as an empty canard. This is a king that *will kill her.* We certainly have been given no reason to believe that he would not.

And so that is when & where Rumpelstiltskin comes in, enters the tale proper, although we have not yet in the narrative been vouchsafed his appellation, nor have we been told wherever it is that he is coming from. His true name we know from the outset, of course, it being the title of the story. So what is truly interesting about the tale is how we will discover where he actually lives, and what he does there, and something more about him. And it will be the miller's daughter who will find these things out, and it is *how* she shall do this which is what the tale is really all about.

Illustration by John B. Gruelle

Then the little man said,
"What will you give me if I spin it for you?"

"My necklace," said the girl.

This is the economical exchange of dialogue (two lines) that will set up the recurring plot device of the story, which is: *The Bargained-for-Transaction*.

To be sure, this is not the very first transaction of the tale. In the very second sentence of the story, the foolish miller effectively offered up his daughter to the king, remember, *to give himself consequence*. And the king, albeit unilaterally, states the conditions of a very high stakes deal upon the arrival of the miller's daughter: she must give him a room full of spun gold by the next morning, in exchange for her life.

But the little man's invitation to a trade, and the poor girl's offer of her necklace, is the tale's very first *bargained-for-transaction*. It seems, certainly, to be a drastically *imbalanced* exchange: any necklace possessed by a poor miller's daughter would likely be a trinket, costume jewelry, and hardly fair value for a room full of spun gold.

Perhaps. But consider this: *how would a poor miller's daughter come into possession of even a trinket of a necklace?* And here we have to speculate, admittedly, on the evidence of what has *not* been said in the story: to wit, the glaring omission of any mention in the tale of the poor girl's *mother*. Think about it: there is no wife waiting at the mill to berate the stupidity of her boastful husband; no mother there to protect and hide her beautiful daughter, perhaps deep in the Black Forest, before setting out on trail and path and road to the castle, to plead for her child's life before the king. The poor girl's mother is unaccountably absent from the story, and from her life. We have already surmised, I think, that the girl is motherless — (and can even imagine that her mother perished in the travail of her first and only childbirth, given that the girl is the miller's *one beautiful daughter*) – and so the miller's daughter has come into possession of the necklace by inheritance, intestacy, forfeit; the necklace likely so worthless that the craven miller let her have it, even maybe told her to wear it, dressing her up for the king.

So there is arguably some inexplicit textual support for concluding that the necklace must be an heirloom, and hence precious to the beautiful girl, a token of her departed mother. But she gives it up, bartering this tangible connection to her dead mother in exchange for her own life.

It is the first step she will take in leaving childhood behind; separating from the memory of a parent and moving forward into her own life, and ultimately becoming a mother, herself. So this is not a trade of a mere trinket for a room full of gold. The beautiful girl is on the side of life, chooses breath and heartbeat and sex over death and memory, offers a valued heirloom for the chance to live and give life.

Quid pro quo.

⋆RUMPELSTILTSKIN⋆

Illustration by Walter Crane

The little man took the necklace,
seated himself before the wheel,
and whirr, whirr, whirr!

Three times round and the bobbin was full,

then he took up another, and whirr, whirr, whirr;
three times round, and that was full;

and so he went on till the morning,
when all the straw had been spun,
and the bobbins were full of gold.

What a picture, here! Filmic. Dissolve to dissolve, in cinematic vignettes of the mysterious *little man*, working away all night, with a crisp & proficient quickness, at the wheel. The magical worker, cross-cut with stationary camera-shots of the miller's daughter: standing and gazing at him, and then seated and heavy-lidded in the dead of the dark night, and then perhaps laid down and curled up and asleep in the tailings of the straw at dawn, the little man gone, and waking to find the gold glistening all around her.

Horrorshow! Yes, because this truly *would* be a horror, a shock to the Ludwig von Mises and to the acolytes of Ayn Rand and to the Ron and Rand Pauls, and to the whole school of Austrian Economists, all of whom have so consummately believed in the supremacy of the gold standard. *Because there is nothing perpetual and permanent about the relative value of gold.*[15]

---

[15]   Prediction: someday, surely, some deep cleft in the ocean floor will yield the pure *Au* element, hard & heavy & glowing yellow, in abundant cart-loads. Or it will be mined on an asteroid and imported in rocket cargoes. Or, indeed, gold will finally be transmuted from lead, or even straw, by some process of fusion or fission. Somehow or other, gold will become abundant, and thus cheap.

It is at this point in *Rumpelstilzchen* that the machinery of the plot is cranked up and wheeling in its first revolution. The miller's daughter will awake without the necklace, and the little man vanished, but with gold all around her. She has bargained for the labor of the little man, and may live another day, but none of the gold will be hers. By right, it will all belong to the king, on account of his ownership of the straw, the spinning wheel, and the room where it was spun. And so, regarding this arrangement, a segue, here:

A younger contemporary of the Grimms would base an entire utopian social system upon his conclusion that such an economic order is fundamentally unjust. Karl Marx was born in 1818, in the Rhenish city of Trier, then recently liberated from the French, albeit by the Prussians. Like the Grimms, he was a student of the great German jurist and legal scholar Friedrich Karl von Savigny. But unlike the Grimms and Savigny, Marx was an internationalist, in a land that had yet to become even a nation. And Marx, I think, can help us understand what is really going on in *Rumpelstilzchen*.

Young Karl Marx

At sunrise came the king, and when he saw the gold he
was astonished and very much rejoiced,
for he was very avaricious.

He had the miller's daughter taken into another room
filled with straw, much bigger than the last, and told
her that as she valued her life
she must spin it all in one night.

Karl Marx was a crank. Publicly a curmudgeon and a strictured thinker, wrong about a lot of things that, being who he was, and when, he did not foresee. But Karl Marx was also an idealist, and he liked children. His own children,[16] and grandchildren, anyway. His youngest daughter Eleanor, born a year before the 1857 publication of KINDER-UND-HAUSMÄRCHEN, recalled for posterity that he was a wonderful playmate, giving her piggy-back rides and, while writing THE EIGHTEENTH BRUMAIRE OF LOUIS BONAPARTE, letting himself be harnessed to pull "his three little children who sat behind him on chairs, cracking their whips."[17] *Ouch.* But, according to Eleanor's reminiscence, her father "also read aloud to his children" — "the whole of Homer, the NIBELUNGENLIED, Gudren, DON QUIXOTE, the THOUSAND AND ONE NIGHTS"–and Shakespeare. "Shakespeare was our family Bible, and before I was six I knew whole scenes from Shakespeare by heart."[18]

---

[16]   At least his *legitimate* children, anyway. Marx's bastard son Frederick, sired with the family's maid Helene Demuth in 1851, was given out to foster care and was never acknowledged by his father — (Friedrich Engels claimed paternity at the time, and not until he was on his deathbed, in 1895, did Engels disclose that Marx [dead, himself, in 1883] was Frederick's father; *Fred* having meanwhile grown up in London to become a mechanic and a good union man and a moderate labourite, never marrying, and deceased in 1929) — a sad orphan tale, full of tragic irony, which the Grimms or Hans Christian Andersen would have well understood, in full. THE PORTABLE MARX, Eugene Kamenka, ED., 1983, pp. xviii, cii.

[17]   Eleanor Marx-Aveling, *Karl Marx – Lose Blatter*, in OSTERREICHISCHER ARBREITER – KALENDAR FÜR DAS JAHR 1895, pp. 51-54, *cited in* MOHR UND GENERAL, pp. 269-79; *as quoted and attributed in* THE PORTABLE MARX, Eugene Kamenka, ED., 1983. Admittedly, the dates don't seem to square, here: THE PORTABLE MARX gives the year of Eleanor's birth as 1856, and puts the publication of EIGHTEENTH BRUMAIRE in 1852. Certainly, though, Marx might well have read *Rumpelstilzchen* to his grandchildren.

So, if we imagine Marx reading *Rumpelstilzchen* to his progeny — (a quite likely historical possibility, given the time-lines and his recitations of the NIBELUNGENLIED and the THOUSAND AND ONE NIGHTS) — if we can imagine this much, we must also picture Marx pausing right here in the tale, at the description of the *very avaricious* king, for a side lecture to his brood on his own budding theory of *Primitive Accumulation*.

Marx, typically, never provided a straightforward, succinct definition of *Primitive Accumulation*. It was his explanation of that primogenitive *leg-up* whereby, early-on, certain astute persons lifted a haunch to get themselves astride a heap of ill-begotten capital, thereby overlording their persons above everybody else:

> This primitive accumulation plays in political economy about the same part as original sin in theology . . . . In actual history, it is notorious that conquest, enslavement, robbery, murder, briefly force, play the great part . . . . The so-called primitive accumulation, therefore, is nothing else than the historical process of divorcing the producer from the means of production. It appears as primitive, because it forms the pre-historic stage of capital and the mode of production corresponding with it.[19]

The avaricious king of *Rumpelstilzchen* seems, at first, explicable in the context of Marx's theory of *Primitive Accumulation,* for how indeed does one get to be *king?* By being ruthlessly avaricious. Opportunistic, aggrandizing, brutal. And certainly this king is all that. And following this tangent, in frolic and detour, there is an argument for *Rumpelstilzchen* as an illustration of the process of "divorcing the producer from the means of production." The king, after all, *owns* the spinning wheel, and will be the beneficiary of the wealth that is produced and accumulated thereby.

---

[18]   Ibid. *See, contra,* KING LEAR, Act I, sc. i. ("[Y]et was his mother fair, there was good sport at his making, and the whoreson must be acknowledged."). Eleanor Marx died by suicide in 1898; her older sister Laura, and her French socialist husband Paul, together killed themselves in 1911. THE PORTABLE MARX, Eugene Kamenka, ED., 1983.

[19]   DAS KAPITAL, chapter 26, *The Secret of Primitive Accumulation.* THE PORTABLE MARX, pp. 462-464.

But the little man never gives up his trade secret of spinning gold from straw, and the king never achieves any power over the magical worker, nor even learns of his role in the tale. Instead, it is the miller's daughter who is put under duress, and exploited, with the king always at this one remove from the means of production. In Marxist terms, then, the miller's daughter is relegated to being a mere intermediary between the laborer and the primitive accumulator. And so, since the girl will emerge as the heroine of the tale, a Marxist economic analysis does not suffice to explain what is really going on here. This is not a polemic about the evils of primitive accumulation and the exploitation of labor, nor an apology for the deposition of unjust kings

That said, the brothers Grimm, it is fair to say, would not have liked this king. He was, after all, an exponent of everything that the Grimms were up against in Germany: the despots of fractured principalities — barons, earls, archbishops — whomever had the local franchise for bilking the peasantry, probably at the point of pike staffs. There is no sympathy here for the much burdened sovereign, who (after all) presumably had an army to be paid, and retainers, and all the petty expenses of running the biggest household around, to keep up appearances.

Rather, we see the king at sunrise, giddy with his ill-gotten wealth, immediately having the poor girl ushered to another room full of straw — "*much bigger than the last*" — to face her second trial. But the king now shows some glimmer of appreciation for her abilities, and future possibilities, since he is not so brutal so as to bluntly say again to her, as he did before, that unless she spins all the straw into gold before morning, "thou shalt die." His phrasing has changed, gentled: "*as she valued her life she must spin it all in one night.*" This is no less an ultimatum, perhaps, but it has now been put in affirmative terms, leaving out the unequivocal guarantee that she will certainly be killed if *all* the straw is not spun into gold by morning.

To Marx, a distinction without a difference. But *different*, nonetheless.

The girl did not know what to do,
so she began to cry, and then the door opened,
and the little man appeared and said,

"What will you give me
if I spin all this straw into gold?"

"The ring from my finger," answered the girl.

So the little man took the ring,
and began to send the wheel whirring round,
and by the next morning
all the straw was spun into glistening gold.

This is the second *bargained-for-transaction* of the tale, and it commences with an averment that makes us wonder about the fallibility of our narrator; to wit, that *the girl did not know what to do*. Certainly the girl *does* know what to do, since she begins to cry, which is exactly what prompted the magical little man to so mercifully appear in the first place. So now, in this second room full of straw, this second time around, we can imagine the girl with one tear-bleared eye agaze at the door, which predictably *does* open, just as before, to reveal Rumpelstiltskin there again in the threshold, and again offering to spin all the straw into gold. But, of course, for something in return.

The price, this time, will be *the ring from my finger*. Again, as with the trinket necklace, probably costume jewelry. A token. But a token of what? And here, once more, we have to speculate —   but how would a poor miller's daughter have come into possession of a *ring*?

After all, she is just a *girl*, and *poor*. We can, I think, rule out that such a girl, to all appearances an innocent and without dowry, could have received the ring from some former suitor of her own. The ring, like the necklace before it, must be something that she has *inherited.*

So, if we suppose that the ring is another heirloom from her mother, as we probably ought to do, then this is undoubtedly the dead mother's *wedding ring.* Because when we read of millers in the Grimms' tales — dull & greedy & plodding & craven — the conclusion follows that it is quite out of character for a miller to give away *anything* unless it is something he must do, to get something in return, like a wife. And so this is where the ring must have come from.[20] For how else would the wife of a miller get a *ring,* and how else could her daughter have come into possession it?

It is this ring that, *as she valued her life,* the girl offers to the little man, who takes it in trade. And so her bartering of it, for her own life, must be of some significance. For if the trading of the bequested necklace can be understood as the girl's acknowledgement of her separation from her departed mother, then the giving up of a wedding ring betokens her severance and parturition from both parents — the ring being the symbolic link of their union — and in her surrendering of it, the girl lets go of not only the last tangible remembrance of her mother, but she also, as well, gives up on the father who cannot help her now, has deserted her. She is orphaned.

In this first part of the tale, there are three *bargained-for-transactions* between the girl and *Rumpelstiltskin.* This is the middle one, and it is arguably here where we first get a glimpse of how the girl, until now an abject and clueless and slobbering waif, may yet turn out to be the heroine of the tale. Because this is where she comes out fully on her own, comes to the cusp of childhood's end and must take the next step, to enter upon the unmapped territory of adulthood.

---

[20]   Notably, yet another *transaction;* this one pre-dating the tale proper.

Joseph Campbell, speaking of *the hero* in a television interview that he gave after he had retired from the last of his professorships, said this:

> But then, [heroism] can be seen also in the simple initiation ritual, where a child has to give up his childhood and become an adult — has to "die" you might say, to its infantile personality and psyche and come back as a self-responsible adult — a fundamental experience that everyone has to undergo. We're in our childhood for at least 14 years, and then to get out of that . . . posture of dependency, psychological dependency, into one of psychological self responsibility requires a death and resurrection. And that is the motif of the hero journey — leaving one condition, finding the source of to bring you forth in a richer or mature or other condition.[21]

It may be possible to make too much of this next observation, push it too far, put too fine a point on it. But notice that, upon on the occasion of their first meeting, Rumpelstiltskin's first words to the girl, and in the tale, were *Good evening, miller's daughter.* This second time around, the little man does not address her in terms of her parentage, and indeed omits any mention whatsoever of her status. She is, appropriately in this middle encounter, between states and without status, neither child nor adult, *liminal.*

The little man accepts the offer of the ring, and spins all the straw in the room into gold, *glistening.*

---

[21] Joseph Campbell, *The Power of Myth*. PBS series, interview with Bill Moyers, 1988. The series is marred by Moyers and his pre-scripted questions, pitched like follow-ups but typically missing whatever point the professor has just been trying to make — the interviewer delivering the canned lines as if in a state of rapt happiness, blissed-out, with his clenched grin and an eyebrow arched in affected bemusement — oblivious and unembarrassed and appearing to believe that he is much smarter than he obviously is, and that this is all looking seamless.

Moyers, for many years now a public television journalist and interviewer, or commentator, or whatever, has enjoyed decades on PBS posing as the scourge of hypocrites and plutocrats and oligarchs; the very picture of grandmotherly liberal piety, in aviator's glasses. This, despite the fact that "Bill" Moyers has somehow gotten away with never permitting *himself* to be authoritatively interviewed about his own very questionable activities in the U.S. presidential administration of Lyndon Baines Johnson — even refusing (at this writing) to be interviewed even by LBJ's still-living but elderly prodigy of a biographer, Robert A. Caro. Which is, as Moyers might insinuate about anybody else, shameful.

The king was rejoiced beyond measure at the sight,
but as he could never have enough of gold,
he had the miller's daughter taken into a still larger
room full of straw, and said,

"This, too, must be spun in one night,
and if you accomplish it you shall be my wife."

This is the third and final of the trials that the king will put to the girl — and, in keeping with the *Rule of Three*, it is here, in its third iteration, that the terms of the heroine's ordeal are radically changed.[22] For no longer is the punitive threat of execution, explicit or not, held over the girl's head. Instead the king, *rejoiced beyond measure at the sight* of so much gold, rather hastily presents the girl with what, at first, sounds like a great opportunity: upon the delivery of this last (albeit biggest) room full of gold, she will become his wife — and will thereby rise in status to the rank of *Queenhood* – quite a leap across a good many class hurdles for a "poor miller's daughter."

But it should not be overlook'd that, whether threat or promise, this most recent of the king's decretals is still cast in unilateral terms, imposed, and is thus yet another ultimatum. For the girl is not free to refuse this last challenge, nor even to decline the king as her *husband* in the event that, upon the morrow, he should open up the door of this third and largest room to find still more gold heaped up and glistening there, spun from all the straw.

---

[22]   This sentence, as originally written, was bookmarked for the later insertion of a supporting footnote, on the pretty fair guess that somebody, somewhere, must have certainly at some time or another published a book or put out a monograph or (at least) flogged off a doctoral dissertation entitled something like *The Rule of Three in Folk Tales* – or myths or fairy tales or scriptures or whatever – since the *motif* of the hero/ine surmounting three variations of a given task or temptation or trial is so pervasive in folk & scriptural literatures so as to suggest all kinds literary theories, ethnographic and psychoanalytic and archetypical. Sure enough, the most cursory of computer researches, run today under the rubric of *Rule of Three*, turns up Vladimir Propp's MORPHOLOGY OF THE FOLKTALE (1928), availability (at this writing) unknown.

For, he thought,
"Although she is but a miller's daughter,
I am not likely to find anyone richer
in the whole world."

Wrong.

Here, in this very first *aside* of the tale,[23] the previously fearsome king is exposed as somebody who is plainly fallible, can be played false. Because even a marginally attentive child, upon hearing the story for the very first time ever, by now knows something that the king certainly does not: it is the *little man* (about whom the king knows nothing at all) who has been all along spinning the straw into gold. And so, whatever other earthly gratifications the king may get by making the miller's daughter his wife, *we* know that riches of gold will not be among them.

Probably, for this avaricious king, a sharp disappointment. And, looking ahead, we may well worry for the girl when the king, wed in haste, discovers his mistake and repents his over hasty promise to make the indigent miller's daughter his queen. *She's in big trouble,* we may think. And maybe, too, *She has it coming.*[24]

But is the king really being cheated? In legal terms, has the miller's daughter made any fraudulent representation, so as to induce the king's reliance

---

[23]   True, in the very second sentence of the tale, the narrator almost immediately departs from the straightforward recitation of outwardly observable facts — *(There once was a miller who was poor, but he had one beautiful daughter)* — in order to depict a character's thinking — (the miller's false boast, made *to give himself consequence,* that his daughter could spin gold from straw). But the king's rationale for making the miller's daughter his wife is the first *explicit* aside in the narrative. And it will soon be followed up by another such aside, disclosing the miller's daughter's own thoughts.

[24]   This is the stuff of old folk ballads, penned to commemorate (and profit by) the fate of some poor unfortunate who has somehow offended the sovereign — poacher or poisoner or cutpurse or attendant-maid pregnant with the king's bastard progeny — narrative songs in rhymed quatrains which, since the earliest days of moveable type, were crudely printed up as broadsides and sold for a ha'penny in the publick squares, often upon the occasion of the miscreant's hanging. *See, e.g.,* MARY HAMILTON, and the like.

and result in his injury? Has she said *anything* that would render voidable the king's contractual promise, or that would be actionable in tort, or even constitute the grounds for a royal divorce, or at least an annulment? Of course not: whenever in the presence of the king, the girl has been silent, utterly. She never claims to have spun the gold from the straw.

But did she have some *duty to speak,* so as to set the king straight on the facts? This is an often convenient legal theory; one of those utile inventions of the common law, of dubious validity. But again, no. Because, curiously, this time around, the king has omitted to stipulate just *who* must turn the straw into gold. Instead, he says, *This, too, must be spun . . . .*

Which is interesting, as least syntactically. Because when the king put the miller's daughter in the first room, he was very clear in stating that she would die "if by the early morning *thou* hast not spun all this straw into gold." And before shutting her up in the second room, he was just as explicit about the terms of the trial, specifying that *she* must spin all the straw into gold, in one night. But notice that in this third iteration, the king has neglected to require that the girl personally spin the straw into gold, because he has instead employed that bane of second-rate pedagogues and grammarians: *the passive voice.* And, to the delight of them and their ilk, he will *pay* for it.

Walter Crane's King Midas

As soon as the girl was left alone,
the little man appeared for a third time and said,

"What will you give me if I spin the straw for you
this time?"

"I have nothing left to give," answered the girl.

"Then you must promise me
the first child you have after you are queen,"
said the little man.

Cut to the chase. No more with the miller's daughter knelt down at the halted wheel and weeping at the hopelessness of her situation, as in the dwindling twilight of the first night; nor her crying begun again with one eye fixed to the door, as must have happened on the second evening. None of that. *As soon as the girl was left alone, the little man appeared for a third time* – and promptly gets down to the real deal that he has been setting up since before his inexplicable first entrance – *What will you give me if I spin the straw for you this time?* Right to the point. No dancing around *this*.

Her reply is stark: *I have nothing left to give.* Which the little man knows already, and more. He holds both her necklace and the ring, betokening that the girl has lost her mother, has no father she can call upon, is an orphan. She has *nothing* now, except, crucially, an *expectation* – of being wedded to the king, and so bearing the royal progeny. It is *this* that the little man is putting a lien on: the first-born of the union that he alone can bring about.

Congruent with the Rule of Three, this third tableaux in the triptych of the girl's encounters with the little man looks radically different than the previous two scenes. Before, we pictured the poor girl as supine and tearful, her head bent and the little man at eye-level, maybe seen through the spokes of the unspinning wheel. But now she is standing — hasn't had the chance to sit down or well up with tears — and so she is bargaining on her feet, clear-eyed and with picture-perfect good posture, squared off and looking down upon the little man.

Moreover, as before with the king, the terms of the deal that the girl is presented with in this third iteration have undergone a *qualitative* change. The king went from putting the girl under the ban of death, twice, to offering her the banns of marriage. Tritely put, but true. And the little man has gone from taking two paltry trinkets in trade to making his play for a *child*. This is a big difference, and it is the first time that the little man has named his price, dictated the terms of a prospective deal. A necklace and a ring, whatever their talismanic significance to the girl, are things of fixable value; whereas the worth of a *child* is obviously incalculable, of an entirely different order of magnitude.

But something else is happening here, too, which becomes obvious when the plot mechanics are charted out, categorizing what each of the parties receives, per transaction:

#	Rumpelstiltskin	Miller's Daughter	King
1.		Deliverance from death	Gold
2	Necklace	Straw/gold	
3		Deliverance from death	+ Gold
4	Ring	+ Straw/gold	
5		Queenhood	++Gold; Wife; *Promise* of unlimited wealth
6	*Promise* of child	++Straw/gold (Queenhood)	

Whereas the first four transactions are straightforward trades, the final two bargains introduce the element of *promise*: the king's assumption that marrying the miller's daughter entails the promise of unlimited wealth, and the little man's more explicit extraction of the girl's promise of the firstborn child.

In legal terms, the element of a *bargained-for-promise* is the difference between a simple swap and a *contract*. And just as there was a preliminary question as to whether the marriage contract between the king and the girl was voidable on the grounds of *fraud in the inducement* — (which it was not, the girl neither having made any false representation nor having any duty to speak) — so, too, there is the issue of the enforceability of the contractual promise of the future queen's child. This time, an obvious legal challenge would be that the girl was under *duress* when she entered into the contract to deliver the child — except that she plainly wasn't. Unlike her dire situation during the first two trials, the girl is not under the threat of death when, for a third time, the little man offers to spin the straw into gold. Rather, she now stands to substantially benefit from his labor, by becoming queen.

Other legal theories, in addition to misrepresentation and duress, may avail to set aside a contract. Ultimately, the only one that will be arguably applicable to *Rumpelstiltskin* is that an agreement can be deemed null and void on the ground that it is *unconscionable*. And we may, reflexively, be quick to say that any deal by a mother to trade her child is *patently* unconscionable.

But *why?*

Illustration by H.J. Ford

"But who knows whether that will happen?"
thought the girl; but as she did not know what else to
do in her necessity, she promised the little man
what he desired, upon which he began to spin,
until all the straw was gold.

So far, there have been three (3) times when the king has put the miller's daughter to the test, and three (3) bargained-for-exchanges between the little man and the girl. Congruent with the *Rule of Three*, shouldn't there be a third three of something else?

Well, of course, there is. For now we have a third instance of the narrator providing a character's inner motivation for a decisive act: the girl's rationalization that *Who knows whether that will happen?* This follows the narrator's initial disclosure of the miller's impetus for his empty boast (*to give himself consequence*) and the king's incentive to promise her marriage (*I am not likely to find any one richer in the whole world*) — and like both of those, this third depiction of a character's thinking displays what we can see to be obviously faulty reasoning. For there is no cause to doubt that the miller's daughter will, as the king has promised, marry and become queen; and, since everything that the little man has promised has so far come to pass, there is every reason to believe that his prediction that the queen will have a child will come true. *We* certainly know where this is going, and that the girl will surely become a mother.

So is the girl being disingenuous here? And isn't she rationalizing a bad bargain because *in her necessity* she does not know what else to do? We have already seen that she is no longer operating under the necessity of having to barter with the little man in order to save her own life, since the king, in this third trial, is not threatening her with death. Shouldn't the girl, too, see that she is destined to become a mother if she strikes the bargain with the little man, but that she is not under any compunction to do so?

Well, no. Because at this point in the story, she is a still a *girl*. A child herself. And although a child cannot truly *know* that she will succeed in becoming a wife and a mother, and cannot entirely comprehend how she will do it nor imagine all that will be required of her, she still nevertheless *must* make the transition from childhood to adulthood. And *this* is the necessity that she is now in: she has to *grow up*.

So it is here where she embarks on her own heroic quest, unsure that she can accomplish it but compelled to make the attempt. And this is what makes her the prospective heroine of the tale, and its central character. Her thinking, at this point, may be immature and confused, but there is nothing disingenuous about it.

Since the teller of the tale knows what the miller, the king, and the miller's daughter are all thinking, we might assume that we have, here, the typical *omniscient narrator*. The authoritative third-person author, once-removed, knowing all. But maybe not. This is a story that constantly plays with the idea that its personages have only a limited knowledge about their world, whether they know it or not: the plot is driven at every turn by a character who must decide, and act, despite the lack of some critical piece of information — be it how to spin gold from straw (the miller's daughter) or that a little man has in fact been spinning it (the king). The tale will end with the revelation that not even the magical little man knows all, and can be fooled. And one trick of the tale may be on *us*: that even its teller is not quite the abstract and all-knowing narrator that we have been led to expect.

And when in the morning the king came
and found all done according to his wish,
he caused the wedding to be held at once,
and the miller's pretty daughter
became a queen.

With the wedding being held *at once*, it is doubtful that the king paused to summon the miller to the castle to give the bride away. Probably not. There is no mention as to whether the miller was in attendance at the nuptials, and either way, it doesn't matter: the *miller's pretty daughter* has abruptly become *a queen*. She can never go back to her father, or live at the mill and sit idly by the millpond, or confide in the companions of her girlhood, as she must have once done. Rather, she is now suddenly the wife of a king, and will live in his castle, and will command servants and messengers, instead of having her childhood friends to rely upon. Clearly, a radical change in her status. And, in the context of the Grimms' tales, this is regarded as a *good* thing.

But she hasn't *earned* it, yet. So the news about her marriage, pretty bride and all, really serves only to demarcate the first and second parts of the tale. For to be truly a heroine, she still has to adultly meet and surmount a final and greatest test, as all the Grimms' protagonists have to do: drawing upon whatever assets she chances to possess, and confronting the enchantment or curse that most threatens her, and outwitting it. Her husband the king will be of no help to her in meeting this final challenge, and this is the last we shall hear of *him* in the tale. Exit the king.

She will be given a year, and be called the queen all that time, with all the rights and responsibilities and privileges attendant thereto. And then she will be tested.

End of the First Part.

Part 2

Queen

In a year's time she brought a fine child into the
world, and thought no more of the little man;
but one day he came suddenly into her room, and said,

"Now give me what you promised me."

It must have been a whirlwind of a year, of sexual initiation and quickening
with child and being flattered by courtiers and treated like a queen all that time,
for her to have actually forgotten the terrible & fateful promise that she made
to the little man. Out of sight, out of mind. Hard to believe. But, as we shall
see, we have it on quite good authority – Our Narrator – that she actually *did*
think no more of the little man. Maybe she repressed it.

Anyway, he re-enters. Another magical appearance, without any flash of
light or puff of smoke, but *suddenly*. Right into the room, the regal chambers,
mysteriously past the sentinels & sentries & the chamberlain. And the little
man is blunt, doesn't pause for introductions or any small talk, gets
immediately down to the business at hand, cuts right to the bone. *Now give me
what you promised me.*

In legal terms, the little man is demanding the queen's performance of
her promised obligation under their contract. It is a *legal* claim, albeit not
reduced to writing. But in this pre-literate province of the future Germany, any
defense founded upon anything like the England's 1677 Statute of Frauds must,
well, founder. A *fine child* cannot be valued in monetary terms, nor is it a parcel
of land, and its gestation transpires within a span of nine months – well short
of the year referenced in the Statute of Frauds.[25] For a defense to the little
man's claim, the queen will have to better than that.

---

[25]   Per BLACK'S LAW DICTIONARY (West Publishing Co., 1990 edition), the Statute of Frauds provides
"that no suit or action shall be maintained on certain classes of contracts or engagements unless there shall be
a note or memorandum thereof in writing signed by the party to be charged or by his authorized agent (e.g.,
contracts for the sale of goods priced at $500 or more; contracts for the sale of land; contracts which cannot,
by their terms, be performed within a year, and contracts to guaranty the debt of another)."

We have previously ruled out the legal defense that the girl was acting under *duress* when she agreed to remit her child to the little man — (she was *not*, then, under the threat of death; hence, no duress) — and now we must concede that any theory based on *fraud* cannot avail her. The little man has been, so far, flatly up-front about what he will do, and for what in return. But, like the queen, we recoil at the thought of handing over an infant babe into the clutches of this odd and mystifying stranger. It will turn out that she *does* have a solid legal defense; but, acting without the assistance of counsel, the queen will miss it. Entirely. And the little man, quite the wiser, will extinguish this defense by a stratagem which, to the queen, looks like *mercy*. In fact, Rumpelstiltskin is something of a con-man.

And one more thing, before we get to that: notice that we have not been told whether the *fine child* is a baby girl or a baby boy. In this place, at this time, a distinction of great and political consequence. For if she had brought into the world a male child, he would be the heir presumptive to the throne, the potential regent of the kingdom. But, if a female, the child would be merely the bargaining chip for some alliance, with the burden of dowry.

The story leaves this quite significant fact out, and I think for a reason. Those little boys hearing the tale, who before now may have been rooting for the exciting and magical little man, may reconsider upon the prospect of being, as a babe, actually delivered unto his sole custody. For little boys, too, need their mothers. Then again, it could be a baby girl. Doesn't matter.

The queen was terrified greatly,
and offered the little man
all the riches of the kingdom
if he would only leave the child;
but the little man said,

"No, I would rather have something living
than all the treasures of the world."

Scary stuff. The Aristotelian shock of recognizing that what has really been driving the tale all along has never been *gold*, after all, but *the child*. Not sterile & inorganic *riches* but *something living*, valued by the little man above *all the treasures of the world*. And so gold has been a mere *McGuffin* in the tale: a comparatively worthless thing that has been the mistaken objective of the contestants. The little man really wants a *child*, something incalculably more valuable than transmuted metal. This is where he has been heading since before his first entrance: what he would *rather have*, more than anything and everything else in the world.

Because the little man, by himself, may be able to spin out his nuggets of white gold from shafts of straw, fed through his hand and pumping the treadle, but he cannot accomplish the making of a *child* by the performance such solitary labors. That is quite something else, beyond his masturbatory magical powers, beyond *him*, so strange & stunted & mateless. And so he must scheme and plot and barter with a pretty & fecund & mated female to obtain and have, all to himself and for himself, *something living*.

Why? What does he intend to do with the child, once he has it? We do not know, and neither can the queen. The little man has no social status in this feudal world, is neither lord nor vassal, nor a member of any guild. In a tale wherein the characters are denominated throughout in terms of their societal roles (miller, king, miller's daughter), the little man is conspicuously without any such referent. He is outside society, subject to nobody. The queen, without the benefit of being told the title of the tale at the outset, does not even know his name. He is a stranger, and strange. Suspect & sinister. The idea of handing over a vulnerable babe to him is abhorrent, and the imagination quails at envisioning what he may want the child *for*.

Is it going too far, then, to see the little man as that archetypical outsider of European history, alien & unfathomable & evil — *the Jew?* Have we not heretofore imagined him as hook-nosed and dark, and distrusted his trick of spinning of gold from straw as ill-gotten wealth, and regarded him as crafty and subversive and a sharp dealer? And now there is his staked claim to a *child,* hearkening back to the ancient Blood Libel, the superstition that Jews murder children to use their blood in religious rituals and for the baking of matzos for Passover — the blood of Christian infants being particularly prized.

True, the Grimms were elsewhere more explicit in KINDER-UND-HAUSMÄRCHEN when reporting folktales about the purported evils of this alien race — stories which relish in recounting the cruelties visited upon the venal and cheating Jews.[26] Whether the *little man* is a Jew, or analogous to a Jew, awaits more textual support. Which is, in fact, shortly forthcoming.

---

[26]   In *The Good Bargain* (KHM 7), a bumpkin, lying to the king, claims that a Jew has not lent him the fine coat he is wearing for his appearance at court. "Ah, said the peasant, what a Jew says is always false - no true word ever comes out of his mouth." The king agrees, and has the Jew beaten. An even more sadistic tale, *The Jew in the Thornbush* (KHM 110), recounts the torture of a Jew by a released servant who has set out over hill and dale, and has fortuitously been given a magic gun and an enchanted fiddle. This "honest worker" encounters a Jew admiring the miraculous voice of a songbird perched in a high tree. The servant shoots the bird dead, and it falls down into a thornbush. "All right, you lousy swindler," the worker says, "go and get the bird." But once the Jew is under the bush, the worker is overcome by a "mischievous spirit" and takes out the enchanted fiddle and plays, making the Jew dance, such that "the thorns ripped the Jew's coat to shreds, combed his goatee, and scratched and pricked his entire body." Only when the Jew gives the "good servant" his bag of gold does the fiddler relent. Ultimately, after the Jew goes into the city and seeks redress from a Judge, he is hanged on the gallows for his trouble. The tale is seldom anthologized, for obvious reasons. (Zipes, COMPLETE FAIRY TALES OF THE BROTHERS GRIMM [1987]).

But see, in fairness, *contra*, *The Bright Sun Brings it to Light* (KHM 115), wherein a tailor, who "thrust God out of his heart" and robbed and murdered a Jew, is ultimately brought to justice as the Jew had prophesied in his death throes. It is noteworthy, however, that the tailor is finally undone by the Jew's dying utterance of a fatal curse, indicating that his alien race harbors preternatural and dangerous powers.

Then the queen began to lament and to weep,
so that the little man had pity upon her.

"I will give you three days," said he,
"and if by the end of that time
you cannot tell my name,
you must give up the child to me."

We have had three attributions, so far, as to what personages of the narrative were *thinking*, what motivated them. Miller, king, miller's daughter. All rang true. Now, in this second part of the tale, we are provided an explanation for the motivation of the magical *little man* in proposing his tripartite riddling contest – that he is relenting out of *pity* – and this one, I think, we should distrust.

First, because we are led to distrust everything about the little man. He is beyond the pale, not a part of society, without the responsibilities and obligations of any social role, an outsider. Anything surmised about the little man — and particularly the attribution that he is now acting charitably, out of an impulse to be merciful— feels unreliable, should be warily regarded. He is simply unknowable. And, hence, untrustworthy.

Second, because there is a sound legal basis to reject *pity* as the little man's motivation for proposing this new bargain. And that is because his original offered bargain for the as the yet un-conceived child was made a mere *girl*, who had yet to become a queen & wife & mother, and an adult. And, as a mere child, *the girl* lacked the legal *capacity* to make such a bargain. This is affirmed by the most exalted legal mind of the Grimms' generation — their mentor and friend (who would, in fact, later be in his life one of the young Karl Marx's professors) — Friedrich Karl von Savigny, who wrote this:

> The capacity to act must be judged exclusively at the time of the juridicial fact, in regard to both the facts and to the subsisting law. If, therefore, a minor without guardian concludes a contract, that contract is and remains invalid, even after [s]he has attained full age . . . .[27]

104

We have seen how, by the trading off of the necklace and ring, that the *girl* became *a minor without guardian*. The *juridicial fact*, then, is that she made her bargain with the little man when she was an unprotected and legally incompetent *minor*. The deal she made as a child is, thus, unenforceable — unless the queen, now an adult, can be inveigled into *ratifying* their contract.[28] And this is exactly what the little man snookers her into doing.

This means that Our Narrator is neither omniscient nor entirely reliable, since crediting the little man with the quality of mercy, while failing to recognize his calculated deception, is demonstrably erroneous. So, if we do not have the traditional omniscient narrator, who is telling the tale?

I think that this is a story that a parent tells a child, and that it is the queen who is telling it. Only the queen would know the miller well enough to say why he would so recklessly boast about his daughter, and she would likewise be familiar enough with the ilk of her husband the king to surmise his base motivation for offering to marry her. She knows, too, her own mind. But she cannot begin to guess what cunning and guile the little man is capable of, perhaps to her credit. Instead, she over-estimates the efficacy of her own lamenting and weeping in prompting him upon his first appearance to offer his assistance, and now to propose the riddling contest. Our Narrator *never* recognizes that this magical helper has, all along, been helping only himself. She does, however, now recognize him as her enemy.

---

[27]   Friedrich Karl von Savigny, TREATISE ON THE CONFLICT OF LAWS, § 388 (Wm. Guthrie, trans.), Edinburgh, 1880. The Grimms made the acquaintance of the young professor von Savigny at the University of Marburg in 1803; Marx, decades later, was a student in von Savigny's lecture hall at the University of Berlin, *circa* 1836. We will come back to von Savigny, whose writings were certainly well known to his colleague and later sometime collaborator, the legal scholar and tale collector Jacob Grimm.

[28]   *Ratification* is, in contract law, "the act of adopting or confirming a previous act which without ratification would not be an enforceable obligation, or confirming an obligation by one without the authority to make or do (or who was incompetent at the time the contract was made). The act of ratification causes the obligation to be bind as if such was valid and enforceable in the first instance." BLACK'S LAW DICTIONARY (West Publishing Co., 1990 edition).

Then the queen spent the whole night
in thinking over all the names
that she had ever heard,
and sent a messenger through the land
to ask far and wide for all the names
that could be found.

She does not sleep. Can't sleep. Whether the king is a-snore in the same bedchamber this night, we do not know, but probably he is not. There is an estrangement between this queen & king — certainly she does not confide in the regent, as she might, calling upon his royal powers to save their child — she is alone in this, perhaps feels for good reason that she has to conceal it. Her dilemma is that she must save both herself and her child, and she must marshal all of her own resources to do so.

And this she does, turning first to her own mind & imagination to solve the riddle, but not only that. She draws upon every resource at hand, and under her royal command there is *a messenger*. Whom she sends out to discover any names she might not know, augmenting her own knowledge & experience with the vantage point of another, free to wander the kingdom, of greater scope than her own perspective. This is quite an *adult* thing to do when confronted with a problem. Significantly, the queen does not resort to mere guesswork to solve the little man's riddle, but after mature consideration, adopts the intelligent stratagem of enlisting help.

The messenger is the fifth, and final, personage specifically mentioned in the tale, and the only character who makes his first entrance in its second act. Probably he has not been entrusted with his queen's exact secret, but he has clearly been taken into her confidence, since he does not run and tell the king that she has sent him out, *far and wide*, on the highly suspect errand of gathering *all the names that could be found*. The messenger's fealty is to the queen, and she has chosen wisely: his only actual message will be delivered to her.

And when the little man came next day
(beginning with Caspar, Melchior, Balthazar),
she repeated all she knew,
and went through the whole list,
but after each the little man said,

"That is not my name."

The morning dawns, and sometime during this day will begin (again) the tripartite ordeal of *three days* – the recurring motif of this tale – and so of course it is three names that the queen begins with. They are strange names, although *proper* names, and in fact all three derive all from the same medieval legend. Trivia quiz: see if you can guess which one it is? Answer below.[29]

These first three names are only the beginning. How long must it have taken her to repeat *all she knew*, all the names on her list? Hours and hours, surely, and after each, the same flat answer of the little man, *That is not my name.* Rote, no hints, mechanical. Maddening. By the end of this day, she has exhausted every proper name that is known to her and can be found in the kingdom. She must be truly terrified. But she does not weep and lament, or plead, or give herself up to prayer. Instead, she acts like an adult, and as a queen: she will send out her messenger again, but in a different direction.

---

[29]   Give up? These are the traditional names of the biblical magi, the so-called three wise men, though the bible does not provide their names and nowhere even says how many there were — the supposition that there were three of them was in later legend extrapolated from the three gifts (gold, frankincense, myrrh) that they presented to the infant Jesus. Upon departing the manger scene, the magi were warned in a dream not to report back to Herod, who secretly wished to destroy the child, and instead returned to their own country by another way (Matt. 2:1-12).

So, is it significant that the queen commences the riddling game with these three names? Not so much, I think. Yes, it grounds the queen in the Christian tradition. But this is the only such religious reference in the tale, and it occurs as a mere parenthetical. The queen is not depending upon divine intercession to save her child, but is all the while taking practical measures of her own. A little superstitious invoking of the names of the three magical wise men can't hurt, but this is decidedly not one of the Grimms' many religious tales. The queen, except for the messenger, is on her own.

The second day the queen sent to inquire
of all the neighbors what the servants were called,
and told the little man
all the most unusual and singular names, saying,

"Perhaps you are called Roast-ribs,
or Sheepshanks,
or Spindleshanks?"

But he answered nothing but

"That is not my name."

Sent *whom* to inquire what the servants were called? Why, her messenger, of course. Who by now has searched far & wide throughout the kingdom, beyond the baptismal registries with all the proper names of the kingdom's gentry, to the hear-say reportage of the nicknames of the unlettered peasants and sundry characters inhabiting its hovels, and the messenger now comes back with an inventory of the most bizarre names to be found in the realm — (again, giving us a listing the first *three*) — Roast-ribs & Sheepshanks & Spindleshanks — which seem to be descriptive of the *little man*. We thus imagine him with burnt-oranged & visible ribs, and wooly haunches, and spavined legs, dwarvish & stunted.

A frightening picture, then, of the little man. But *That is not my name.*

We do not imagine him ever inflecting his response, saying *That* is not my name, or That is *not* my name, or That is not *my* name, or That is not my *name.* No. Like the knell of a dull bell, repetitiously intoned and without variation, *That is not my name.*

The third day the messenger came back again,
and said,

"I have not been able to find one single new name; but
as I passed through the woods
I came to a high hill,
and near it was a little house,
and before the house burned a fire,
and round the fire danced a comical little man,
and he hopped on one leg and cried,

"To-day do I bake, to-morrow I brew,
The day after that the queen's child comes in;
And oh! I am glad that nobody knew
That the name I am called is Rumpelstiltskin!"

The messenger enters on the fatal third day and tells the queen that he has not found *one single new name*, when of course, in fact, he has done exactly that. Maybe he is abashed because he has discovered this name by subterfuge: climbing up to the summit of that wilderness hill and trespassing on the little man's territory, peeking out from behind the jack-pines rather than forthrightly making his presence known. Moreover, this trespassing peeper has remained in hiding for long enough to not only watch the *comical little man* dancing about on one leg around a fire, but throughout the entirety of his weird rhyme.

What the messenger has witnessed has all the elements of a *ritual*: the fire burning out in front of the house for no discernable practical purpose, the little man's inexplicable hopping around it, and his crying out of the inscrutable chant. Sacrificial fire, ceremonial dance, sacramental mantra.

But this is not a ritual that is culturally intelligible to the messenger, nor to the queen. It is either the little man's own radically personalized mythological construct,[30] or the rite of some alien race.

---

[30]   Some thirty years ago, in a college thesis, I argued that this bizarre ritual is a manifestation of "schizophrenia." After two decades of working with actual afflicted people as a family court lawyer, I don't agree with my purely social-dynamic portrait of mental illness anymore, nor my conclusion that what the Grimms were getting at in *Rumpelstiltskin* is that the little man an exemplary schizophrenic. Still, it's an alternative reading of the tale, and coherent in theory, and arguable. So, relegated to a footnote, here goes:

[Many persons labeled as schizophrenic] seem to have adopted a highly effective strategy for controlling the cosmos: out of the combination of image and logic they are able to create distinctly personalized and concretized metaphors; these metaphors, in turn, support a meta-cosmic systematization of rituals and symbols which amounts to a lived mythology.

I would posit that the process whereby whole cultures evolve and inhabit mythological structures is different only to the degree that the reification is consensually shared; in order to continue to be meaningful to its various participants, a mass-mythology [such as Christianity] must be comprehensive, flexible, and amendable, or it will be discarded. The individual "schizophrenic" crystallization is, on the other hand, a radically individualized construct; it is hence a closed system, and can be relatively free of anomaly and resistant to change. It is significant that schizophrenics are said to be unable to communicate with one another: their closed constructs are mutually exclusive, paradigms that "talk past" each other. (Kuhn, 1970). At least for some who are labeled as "schizophrenic," then, the adoption of such an autotelic mythology seems to indicate an insular strategy whereby hurt, ambiguity, and unpredictability can be excluded from one's experience of existence, with *relationship* being the price that such an individual must pay for absolute control over the world. [Thus, in *Rumpelstiltskin*] the queen's act of naming has tremendous power because it socially *identifies* the little man. Because he cannot operate in the world except anonymously, the little man *cannot socially exist*. He is a social non-entity who lives in the *woods*. Furthermore, his *ritual*, which consists of hopping about on one leg around a fire, is so personalized that we cannot decode it. Because it is so alien to common conventions, we cannot even interpret from his chant whether he is celebrating the portended arrival of the queen's child because he loves little children or because he likes to eat them. With his lack of social role and status, his indecipherable ritual and chant, and the apparent inability of the omniscient narrator to describe him in any terms except for his physical stature and gender, Rumpelstiltskin is outside the net of relationships that constitutes society. Children, too, are in many ways excluded from the larger society, and child may well identify with a character who is twelve times described as a *little man*. To an adult, however, Rumpelstiltskin's magic and mysteriousness are not appealing, but imply power in unpredictable hands. He is radically *asocial*, and hence a potential threat.

Rumpelstiltskin is, then, a "schizophrenic." His naming by the queen finally puts him under the power of social authority, and this is a condition which destroys him. He cannot allow himself to be socially integrated, for he would lose the total control over the cosmos which he has established through ritual and magic. Consequently when the queen names him, Rumpelstiltskin loses his power over her, and presumably loses his transformational magical power as well. The "little man," a social nonentity with his own set of ritualized conventions, an outsider operating solely in accordance with the dictates of a radically personalized mythological structure, *loses control* when the queen is able to identify him in terms of his distinguishing social referent, his name. His private cosmos, previously inviolable and impenetrable, is destroyed by the queen's ability to manipulate it. And so, with his strategy for absolute control no longer efficacious, Rumpelstiltskin loses control of himself as well, succumbing to what is instantly recognizable, even by a child, as a tantrum.

The queen is a person of status in the body politic; her previous recitation of the traditional names of the three wise men puts her in a Christian cultural context. The little man is quite outside all this. The messenger has to pass through *the woods* to reach his isolated little house; the ritual that he witnesses, together with the chant of baking and brewing with the queen's child coming in, lends further support to the conclusion that the little man is, or is at least analogous to, *the Jew.*

Again, it is true that the messenger never says that the little man is specifically dancing the hora, nor is his baking ever explicitly said to be of matzos, nor is his brewing explained as a beverage recipe for the imbibing of the blood of a Christian infant. But it sure *looks* like it. And it would certainly explain why the bargain between the queen and the little man is not only legally unenforceable in this culture, but why the little man may be derided and persecuted with impunity, as well.

For the legal analysis, we turn again to the most esteemed German legal scholar and jurist of the age, that longtime close colleague of the Brothers Grimm and sometime professor of Karl Marx (remember Marx?) — Friedrich Karl von Savigny. But first, we ought to put Dr. Savigny — one of the founders of the influential "historical school" of German jurisprudence — into the proper historical perspective:

In 1814 the wave of German nationalism inspired by the liberation against Napoleon led the Heidelburg law professor A.F.J. Thibaut to demand a unified civil code for all the German states. Savigny opposed this demand for an immediate codification of German law in a famous pamphlet, *Vom Beruf unserer Zeit für Gesetzgebungund Rechtswissenschaft* (1814: *Of the Vocation of Our Age for Legislation and Jurisprudence*), that started juristic thought along a new path. To Savigny, a hasty legal codification was something to be avoided, since the one essential prerequisite for such a codification was a deep and far-reaching appreciation of the spirit of the particular community. Savigny's jurisprudential perspective was in part inspired by the Romantic movement, which took the form in Germany of a movement harking back to the simplest tribal origins of the German people, to their folk songs and tales and to their distinctive ethos, or *Volksgeist* ("national spirit"). To the Romantics, the national spirit thus became the ultimate datum to be explored in its various manifestations. From this point of view law is not something that can be devised by means of rational formal legislation but rather originates in the unique spirit of a particular people and is expressed spontaneously in custom and, much later, in the formal decisions of judges. In Savigny's classic words, law *"is first developed by custom and popular faith, next by judicial decisions – everywhere, therefore, by internal silently operating powers, not by the arbitrary will of a law-giver."*[31]

We can thus see why the tale-bearing Grimms and the law-giving Savigny were allied in their vision of what German nationalization would look like. The law must hark back to *the simplest tribal origins of the German people, to their folk songs and tales and to their distinctive ethos, or Volksgeist ("national spirit")*. And, once we see just what Savigny had to say about what a legal system based on such tribal values and tales meant for the enforceability of contracts with *Jews*, we can see why Karl Marx — born a Jew, albeit never identifying as such — would reject Savigny's "historical school" for the more rigorous construct of dialectical materialism, and might prefer internationalism to Teutonic nationalism.

For Savigny accepted, without demur, "the many laws which restrict the acquisition of immoveable property by Jews." Savigny explicated that "[i]f our law forbids to Jews the acquisition of landed property, our judges must forbid such acquisition not only to native Jews, but also to those foreign Jews in whose state there is no such prohibition."[31] Savigny also noted, again without registering any exception, that the Jews are "incapable of acquiring rights to debts, except under certain very strict conditions."[33] That was just the way it was, and thus, ever should be.

Savigny's acquiescence to the Jews' lack of capacity to have enforceable property rights was in complete accordance with the "unique spirit" of the German people, "expressed spontaneously in custom" and, "much later, in the

---

[31]   *Friedrich Karl von Savigny* — BRITANNICA ONLINE ENCYCLOPEDIA.

[32]   Friedrich Karl von Savigny, TREATISE ON THE CONFLICT OF LAWS (Wm. Guthrie, trans.), Edinburgh, 1880; §349, *Conflicting Territorial Laws in Different States*. Pettifogging, the professor allowed that "conversely, the foreign state whose law lays no such restriction upon Jews will admit Jews belonging to our state to possess landed property, without respect to the restrictive laws of their personal domicile."

formal decisions of judges." The judiciary should *enforce* such historical folkways, as *rules*. This is, incidentally, a fundamentally *democratic* method of law-making, reflecting the popular will, majoritarian. On the downside, it reflects the deliberate rejection of a logical, pragmatic, and principled law; it is, essentially, the ratification of tribal prejudices. And that is why this book, which you are now reading, is subtitled *Notes for a Law Lecture*. Because we can not only now witness and understand the historical juncture at which the incipient nation of Germany went so tragically wrong, but we should recognize, as well, what is so fundamentally wrong with so much of our own law.[34] But American law, at least, begins with a principled constitution that acts as a check on democratic majoritarianism.[35] Not so with Savigny's vision of the German nation.

In addition to lacking legal capacity to own title to real property and to collect debts, the Jews of Prussia were also lawfully disqualified from holding posts in the civil service. Karl Marx, whose grandfathers on both sides of the family were rabbis, grew up with what must have been a formative experience of such legally sanctioned discrimination. His father, Heinrich Marx, was a respected and prosperous lawyer. However, about a year before Karl was born, Heinrich Marx was baptized a Christian:

> . . . Heinrich entered into baptism only because Prussian legislation forced him to choose between remaining a Jew and remaining a State Legal Counselor in the city of Trier. In 1815, when the Rhineland was reattached to the Prussian Crown, Heinrich had addressed a memorandum to the

---

[33]   ID.; §365, *Status of the Person (Capacity to Have Rights and Capacity to Act)*.

[34]   Take, as one obvious example, the present criminalization of the possession and personal use of a certain variety of natural vegetation; to wit, the plant marijuana. Non-addictive, positively useful in alleviating depression and pain, and, for many people, a help to creativity and relaxation and aspirations to a broader understanding. And yet, federally *illegal*, whereas the much more addictive and destructive and dulling ingestion of grains and fruits, fermented and distilled, *isn't*. This is solely because, historically, alcohol has been the popular recreational drug of the majoritarian *white* people, whereas marijuana has historically been the recreational drug of *black* and *brown* people, minorities. Von Savigny would be perfectly fine with this, but it doesn't make any logical or pragmatic *sense*.

[35]   Indeed, the one lamentable exception that flaws the otherwise principled lawmaking of the U.S. Constitution — the codification of slavery by distinguishing between "free Persons" and "all other persons", and infamously counting the slave as three-fifths of a person — was a concession to the kind of historical custom that Savigny held to be the basis of *all* law.

Governor-General respectfully asking that the laws applying exclusively to Jews be annulled. In the memorandum he spoke of his "fellow believers" and fully identified himself with the Jewish community. In 1816 the President of the provincial Supreme Court recommended that Heinrich and two other Jewish officials be retained in their posts and that the King grant them the special exception made necessary by the the decision to apply Prussian legislation to the Rhineland. The Prussian Minister of Justice failed to recommend such an exception, and Heinrich Marx was baptized.[36]

Eugene Kamenka, the editor of a standard anthology of Marx's writings, further notes that "[s]ome seven years later, on 24 August 1824, the six-year-old Karl Marx (with his five sisters) stood at the baptismal font." Accordingly, "at least one shadow must have hung over the young Karl's earliest years."[37]

Thus, it entirely understandable that Marx, in one of his earliest published writings, rejected the argument that the Jew must give up Judaism in order to be politically and civilly emancipated. Rather, Marx called for "the *emancipation of the state* from Judaism, from Christianity, from *religion* in general."[38] Marx credited the "free states of North America" as being the only place where "the political state has reached its highest development," inasmuch as "the constitution imposes no form of religious faith and no specific religious practice as a precondition for political rights."[39] This, of course, is a flat rejection of Savigny's historical school of law. Marx later went down some rabbit holes (such as *communism*), but we can agree with this atheist grandson of rabbis that the state should not be in the business of dispossessing people of rights on account of religion and race.

---

[36]   THE PORTABLE MARX, Eugene Kamenka, ED., 1983, p. xiv.

[37]   ID., pp. xiv, xiii.

[38]   ID., pp. 97, 100. Marx, Comment on *Die Judenfrage (on the Jewish Question)* by Bruno Bauer, Braunschweig, 1843; published in *Deutsch-französische Jahrbücher,* February 1844.

Every illustration of Rumpelstiltskin in the two centuries since the publication of KINDER-UND-HAUSMÄRCHEN has portrayed him as a dark little man with a hooked nose, often surrounded by heaps of gelt. Look it up; it's uncanny, and disturbing. But we do not have to conclude that Rumpelstiltskin is literally a Jew to see why the bargain he makes with the queen is unenforceable. Under a legal system derived from the *Volksgeist, anybody* who is not a member of the common tribe lacks the capacity to own property, collect debts, achieve status. Jews, Gypsies, homosexuals, Marxists. Rumpelstiltskin, whether a Jew or not, is obviously an *outsider,* and as such he lacks *standing* to demand the performance of his contract for a Christian child — and the *royal* child, at that.

Friedrich Karl von Savigny

---

[39]   ID.

You cannot think how pleased
the queen was to hear that name,
and soon afterwards,
when the little man walked in and said,

"Now, Mrs. Queen, what is my name?"

she said at first,

"Are you called Jack?"

"No," he answered.

"Are you called Harry?"
she asked again.

"No," answered he.

And then she said,

"Then perhaps your name is Rumpelstiltskin!"

How pleased, indeed. For now that the queen knows his name, the little man must forfeit his claim. The messenger's description of Rumpelstiltskin as a *comical little man* indicates that he is regarded as a derisible eccentric once he has been disempowered; the little man is further trivialized when, presently, the queen actually plays a kind of cat-and-mouse game with him before she oh-so-casually drops the name that will provoke him to destroy himself.

The little man begins this third trial, interestingly, by addressing the queen by the first proper appellation that we have yet seen in the tale, *Mrs. Queen*.[40] Having called her by her proper name, he now challenges the queen to reciprocate by guessing his own.

What he does not know, yet, is that this is no longer a riddling game, a matter of guesswork. Such contests are a recurring motif of traditional literature, since at least the myth of Oedipus and the Sphinx,[41] with the protagonist expected to solve the conundrum by reasoned deduction. The queen has not played by the rules, but has learned the little man's name by subterfuge – her spy has spied it out. Now, in addition to cheating, she taunts the little man while harboring her ill-gotten knowledge, is toying with him. In contrast to such odd and obscure names as *Melchior* and *Sheepshanks*, she now cites the prosaic *Jack* and *Harry*[42] before coyly proposing the (of course) *third*, and fatal, name.

This seems vengeful, petty, cruel. We may (and indeed, will) ultimately conclude that the queen has been finally right to do whatever she can, by whatever means necessary, to keep her child. But having made the heroic transition from being a helpless miller's daughter to attaining the status of a resourceful and capable royal adult, Mrs. Queen here abuses her power by abusing the powerless. She takes a malicious pleasure in baiting the little man, is privately gloating about his misfortune. In German, there is a word for this repugnant delight in the plight of another: *schadenfreude*.

But isn't this exactly what the little man deserves? Derision, mockery, persecution? He has no right to own property, collect on a debt, have any legal status. And now he would presume to take the *royal child*? He is a *nobody*. It does not matter that such a *little man* has made the birth of this child possible; that without his intercession, the miller's daughter could not have survived and would never have married the king. *He has been plotting, all along.* A con-man. He is an outsider, a foreigner, an alien.

---

[40]   *Frau Königin* in the original KINDER-UND-HAUSMÄRCHEN.

[41]   *"What animal goes on four legs in the morning, two legs in the afternoon, and three legs in the evening?"*

[42]   *Kunz* and *Heinz*, in the original.

So it is easy to root for the queen as she sets up the little man for his come-uppance; to grin at her little jokes of Jack and Harry, Kunz and Heinz, before she pulls out the rug with her final line in the story: „*Heißt du etwa Rumpelstlzchen?*„

Schadenfreude.

Illustration by Edward Taylor, German Popular Stories, 1823)

"The devil told you that!
The devil told you that!"

cried the little man, and in his anger
he stamped with his right foot so hard
that it went into the ground above his knee;
then he seized his left foot with both his hands
in such a fury that he split in two,

and there was an end of him.

Children, upon first having the tale of Rumpelstilskin read to them, are always shocked and astounded by its denouement. Try it. To a child, this is the story of a generous and magical little man who twice goes out of his way to save the life of a helpless stranger, getting only a simple necklace and a little ring in exchange for all that gold. Even a little child understands that this is hardly a balanced transaction. Finally, with his chance to get his first real reward of the story after enabling the poor girl to marry the *king*, the little man shows mercy. He promises to give up his claim if the queen should guess his name within three days, getting as many guesses as she wants. A riddling game, but the queen does not play by the rules. She never does *guess* the name, but her messenger finds it out by *spying* on the little man while he is singing and dancing. And then the queen even cruelly *teases* him, pretending that she doesn't know that his name is Rumpelstiltskin, being really mean when she finally says it. She has clearly cheated, but Rumpelstiltskin honors his promise. "The devil told you that!" he shouts, and unable to live in a world of such evil and injustice and deceit, he *rips himself in half.*

It's not fair! He doesn't deserve it! And that last part about *ripping himself in half* – you would have to be so *strong* to *rip yourself in half!* You *couldn't* do that! *Could you?* Kids always want to have that last part read to them over and over, grabbing their feet to act out the spectacular gymnastics of it, particularly fascinated with the feat of *ripping themselves in half* as a method of self-annihilation. Or maybe it is the very *idea* of self-annihilation itself which is so fascinating to children, since Rumpelstiltskin is probably the very first literary character they have encountered who is a *suicide,* and maybe the first time they have ever heard of such a thing, considered it as a viable possibility. In psycho-dynamic terms, the little man's ending works perfectly as a cautionary note to the little tantrummer: if you lose control, you could really *hurt* yourself, and be *dead.*[43]

It is thus hard for a child to grasp that Rumpelstiltskin is not the hero of the tale that bares his name.[44] A parent, on the other hand, immediately recognizes the girl/queen as the protagonist of the tale. Her portrait is far more nuanced than the repetitive caricaturization of the merely *little* man: she is consecutively depicted as *beautiful,* perhaps *clever, alone, poor,* in *distress, pretty, terrified, thinking,* and finally, *pleased.* She weeps and laments, thinks and acts, and emerges during the story as a well-delineated and understandable character. The parent, too, watches as the poor miller's daughter negotiates the transition from being a child to adulthood — something that Rumpelstiltskin, who comes to his end in a fatal tantrum, never achieves.

Then there is her dilemma. She is twice put under the threat of death, but it is her third predicament that a parent may envision as a fate even worse than death: losing her child. To a kid, going off with the magical little man may look like an adventure, a nice respite from parental control. To the parent, the idea is horrifying. This does not reflect the distinctive ethos of any specific community or tribe, for even in cultures where parenting is largely outsourced, such as our own, any non-defective parent is terrified at the prospect of a stranger permanently *taking* one's own child. We are, like elephants and whales, a species that is evolutionarily hard-wired to protect our helpless progeny throughout its years of post-gestational immaturity, which is why the threat to take a child from a caring parent is simply *unconscionable.* Such a principle can

---

[43]   In Structuralist terms, incidentally, the conjoining of the little man with his name results in the disjunction of the right and left halves of his body, thereby transforming him into a complimentary duality. See Von Roff, Ivan, *Deconstructing Rumpelstiltskin: A Structuralist Approach to the "Diminutive Troll" Motif in Myth and Folk Tale;* HUDSON RIVER REVIEW (Winter, 1997).

[44]   *Ouch.*

be codified into law without recourse to the *Volksgeist* of any particular tribe or people, and a parent can see that the queen is acting in accordance with a basic tenet of survival.

It is the queen's cruelty to Rumpelstiltskin, her derogation of him as merely a comical little man and her derisive treatment of him, which is problematical even to an otherwise sympathetic adult. This is unnecessary, corrosive, persecutory. A flaw in her character, and a failing of her culture. Not that the Grimms or Savigny probably perceived it as such. Their passionate cause, the unification of the German speaking peoples into a single nation, seemed to them to require the concomitant exclusion of so-called alien elements, non-persons denied the protection of law, who could hence be mistreated with impunity.

But some of the queen's other shortcomings seem more forgivable to us, especially in view of some of the other social conditions then prevailing in the Holy Roman Empire. She willingly marries a capricious and greedy king, for instance, but women in patriarchal societies have often had to ally themselves with such men to in order to survive. And she does not come clean to her husband about how the gold was spun from straw, or that his infant is in jeopardy of being stolen away by a gnome, but this has hardly been our idea of a model marriage; further, we do not know what the king *would* do to the queen, or that he *could* do anything against the power of the magical little man. Finally, the queen's reliance on subterfuge to learn the little man's name is concededly less than honest, but adults know that people in the real world often must act in ways that are not strictly and pristinely correct. The lesson we can still take from *Rumpelstiltskin*, then, is that life's deck is stacked against us, and that in order to prevail we must make some uncomfortable compromises.

And this is what accounts for the difference between a child's and an adult's reaction to the story. The child wants things to be black or white, right or wrong, structurally clear, and simple. A child can be moved to pity by the plight of the poor miller's daughter, while also being confused and ambivalent about how she resolves her problems. To the parent, the queen is a heroine not because she breaks down crying in helpless distress, but because she regains control and acts responsibly and employs whatever power and assets she can command in dealing with an ambiguous and impossible situation. She persists and does what she has to do to survive, and to ensure the survival of her child. She cheats, but cheats death.

After all, this is a story that the *queen* is telling, and she is telling it to her child. It the story of *how you came to be*, and when we read it to our own children, we are telling them the same thing.

Which is this:

> *I had to make some compromises, do some questionable things, to get you into this world. And then, once you were here, I had to protect you, and I somehow kept you sheltered and fed and as safe as I could, and not every thing that I did or had to do in the furtherance of all that am I proud of. But it had to be done, or you would not be here right now, and we would not be having this conversation.*
>
> *For the world can be a dangerous and treacherous place, and life isn't fair. This is not something that you can understand until you grow up, and maybe not until you are a parent yourself, and some people never do.*

The *law* can be fair, and should be made to be so, but *life* is not fair. And if you do not understand this, then you can be in great peril and not even know it. And by then it can already be too late.

And that is the story of Rumpelstiltskin, *and there was an end of him.*

— Finis —

To Hold a Coin Minted

To hold a coin minted
six years before
you were born

gives pause.

You noticed it
was worn and picked it up, and
looking at the date

counted six
years before
you were born.

A nickel and you
have not lived forever.

Cafeteria Poem

"Is anybody sitting here?"
  she asks.
"No," I say. I smile.

"Thanks," she says, and
  drags the chair over
  to the next table.

Clinton Street Incident

I saw a woman on Clinton Street
shrieking at a crying child
who dragged its feet and struggled
and screamed and would not listen –
And so she left it
knelt down on the city sidewalk
and went on a ways

    (I was watching from the temple rooftop
     through the leafless branches
    of an old dead oak)

The child, awkward, rises
and walks the long way, fawnlike
with cowering slowness and glassy eyes
and hesitant stare at the temple steps
where she sits smoking, in a pink sweatsuit
beside a plastic bag of groceries

She gets up, they walk
quiet for a few slow steps
(the child's boot buckle loose
 and skittering across the concrete)
Until she speaks with loud, hard voice
and again the child is lagging.

Original back cover to the 1ˢᵗ edition Anthology of New York State Folk Music

CARDIFF HISTORICAL RECORDINGS

ANTHOLOGY OF

NEW YORK STATE
FOLK MUSIC

WITH REFERENCE RECORDINGS

—— VOLUME ONE ——

BALLADS & SONGS OF UPSTATE NEW YORK

ERIE CANAL SONGS • CARNIVAL BALLADS • NOVELTY TUNES
RURAL BLUES • REELS & JIGS • BARNDANCE WALTZES
WORK SONGS • BROADSIDES • MURDER BALLADS • AN AUBADE

PRODUCED & EDITED BY RUSSELL FOX

CONTENTS

In the Big Inning

T was in the big inning
that Sal told to me
This specimen of
practical poetry:

The most beautiful diamond
a girl can behold
Is not a diamond of stone
in a ring of white gold –

No, the loveliest diamond
that ever could be

Is a grass and sand diamond of green.

In The Big Inning
[Fragment]

"Baseball Dolly"

THOMAS ALVA EDISON (1847-1931), although today remembered as pre-eminently an inventor, was no less a practical mechanic, pioneer industrialist, and a businessman. Motivated by the uniquely American ideal of *making a profit,* Edison's discoveries were made with one famously squinted eye[1] fixed to the manufacture of an ultimate *product,* which people would want to *buy.* An inveterate salesman, and something of a showman, Edison hawked not only his incandescent lightbulb, but the generating stations and power grids that would be required to illuminate it – and thus founded the first investor-owned electrical utility. He devised a moving picture projector, which he patented and pitched as the Kinetoscope – and thereby invented the motion picture industry. But, curiously, upon his invention of the phonograph in 1877, Edison did not at once conceive and seize upon the commercial possibilities of simple reproducible *sound,* in the form of performed & recorded *music,* as a saleable commodity. Edison, in brief, cannot be credited as the father of the modern recording industry — for Edison did not invent *records.*

It is, today, seemingly incredible that the earliest extant commercial recording that can arguably be ascribed to the region of upstate New York is neither a wax cylinder nor a shellac disk, but the mechanical voice of a *talking doll.* But Thomas Alva Edison did not, immediately, foresee the market potential of simple sound recordings, be they vocal renditions of popular songs or the performances of classical orchestras. Instead, Emerson's initial conception of a practical and marketable application of his phonograph was as a mere novelty item, miniaturized and incorporated into a mechanical *toy,* for the entertainment of *children,* specifically *little girls:*

> *Only a month after he had first invented the phonograph in 1877, Edison had already made arrangements to manufacture a smaller version for use in clocks and toys. At the Paris exhibition of 1878, where he*

---

[1] His left eye, in fact. *See, i.e.,* THE WIZARD OF MENLO PARK: A PHOTOGRAPHIC RECORD, 1877-1931, West Cardiff University Press, 1988.

astonished the world with his talking machine, and was awarded the Grand Prize for being "the inventor of the age in which we live," he exhibited this miniphonograph, and a design for a doll from which sound would emerge. . . .

— EDISON'S EVE, Gaby Wood © 2002

Edison's talking dolls, at first, only talked. The Promethian generation recited brief nursery rhymes: HEIDI, manufactured with plaited blonde braids and plaid frock, emitted an eerily shrill and mechanical recitation of *Mary Had a Little Lamb;* and JACK AND JILL, packaged and sold as a complimentary pair, each chanted one of the two quatrains of the well-known Mother Goose rhyme. The mechanisms of the two dolls were activated by the pulling their two strings, in unison.

But by 1890, an Edison doll was yet to *sing,* and Edison himself appears never to have considered such a possibility until it was suggested to him, by way of a somewhat impertinent telegram, sent personally to Edison by George Maynard Ames, a Port Jervis, New York, general goods storekeeper. Upon accepting an exceptionally large consignment of twenty-five talking HEIDI dolls, Ames had the temerity to importune the great inventor to manufacture a *singing* doll, accoutered in baseball costume, to sing *In the Big Inning,* a then-popular song on the sheet music circuit. George Maynard Ames further ventured to recommend a particular child performer to provide the ideal phonographic voice of BASEBALL DOLLY: his twelve-year-old daughter, Mildred Maynard Ames, a prominent chorister in the Port Jervis Episcopal Church, and the shortstop of the local girls' baseball team, the Port Jervis Lady Jack-Rabbits.

Just as significantly, at least insofar as the provenance of this first extant recording of the folk music of upstate New York is concerned, the twenty-two-year-old composer of *In the Big Inning* was Hyman Cohen, a cantor's son from Buffalo, New York. As a budding songster in 1888, Cohen had introduced the tune as a part of his act during his summer stint as a tack-pianist in a Catskill vaudeville house. That autumn, upon the return of the Catskill audiences to New York City, and coincident with the 1888 season's now historic rivalry between the Manhattan Knights and the Queensborough Monarchs, *In the Big Inning* became a popular parlor hit.

Edison, to his credit, was intrigued by the idea of a *singing doll,* and immediately replied by telegraph to Ames, inviting him to submit a design for BASEBALL DOLLY. As George Maynard Ames's subsequent penciled illustration in a surviving letter to Edison reflects, Ames envisioned BASEBALL DOLLY as a brunette pixie, costumed in a pinstriped jumper and equipped with a matching cap.[2] The features of the proposed doll, understandably, bear a striking resemblance to Ames's daughter Mildred, who was promptly invited to Menlo Park to audition Hyman Cohen's *In the Big Inning* for the "Wizard of Menlo Park" himself.

By both extant reports, Edison was charmed by Mildred's rendition of the wildly popular tune, which he phonographically recorded himself in his laboratory on October 11, 1892. However, as a nineteenth century inventor and manufacturer, Edison was also a great respecter of what would much later come to be called *intellectual property.* Upon presenting a working prototype of the doll to his patent attorney, Edison was advised that the melody and lyric of the song *In the Big Inning* was protected by copyright, and was thus subject to royalties. As legend has it, Edison at once spontaneously composed, there in his lawyer's office, and upon the back of an envelope, what he would later charmingly describe as "a fresh new little ditty about the pastime of baseball." Hardly more than a snippet, and apparently the only "practical poetry" and tune that the renowned inventor ever authored, Edison decided to entitle his piece *In the Big Inning,* after being assured by his legal counsel that a mere song title cannot be copyrighted.

By the time that Edison finally completed his second prototype of BASEBALL DOLLY (with a blond coiffure replacing the original brunette braids and banged locks), Mildred Maynard Ames was apparently no longer available to provide the voice for the miniature automaton. The identity of the local child performer whom Edison commissioned to record his own composition for the production model of BASEBALL DOLLY is now, regrettably, unknown.

While the rejected recording of Hyman Cohen's paean to the great game of baseball would be lost to posterity, the mechanical "voice box" of BASEBALL DOLLY would be housed under the zinc breastplates of

---

[2] The BASEBALL DOLLY cap, incidentally, is now a rare and prized item, commanding astronomically high prices on the toy antiquities market. This is presumably because most little girls promptly discarded the cap and swaddled the doll, wanting to mother a more conventional baby dolly. *See illustration, facing page.*

some two thousand mass-produced dolls. Devised to replay the phonographic recording by means of a steel stylus that traveled the groove of a sound pattern impressed into a coiled metal strip, the mechanism proved too fragile to withstand the repeated string-pullings of little children. Nevertheless, although operable working models of the doll are today even rarer than their highly prized baseball caps, four partially working copies of the doll are known to exist. The best of these, fortuitously discovered in the United States Patent Office in 1978, and still capable of reproducing a complete fragment of *Baseball Dolly,* was re-recorded expressly for release as the prefatory selection for the ANTHOLOGY OF UPSTATE NEW YORK STATE FOLK MUSIC.

Lambeth Library of Popular Music, Inc.

Erie Canal Song

Words & music by
Dr. R.E. Reynard

Lambeth Music Company No. 289
75 Mulberry Street, Syracuse, New York

ONLY 25¢

Erie Canal Song

Dr. R.E. Reynard

Canal Song
circa 1927

Although the first edition of its printed sheet music is undated, and the year of its original copyright is thus subject to dispute, folk music scholars are widely agreed that the *Erie Canal Song* could not have been composed any earlier than 1925, the year when the block-limestone embanked route of that historic waterway through the downtown heart of the city of Syracuse was filled in and paved over, as told therein. That the song originated in Central New York is indubitable: its text not only references Syracuse as a city that the canal had *built,* but explicitly ends up with its narrator and his companion, *Sal,* squatting on their heels out on the curbstone of *Erie Boulevard,* today the Salt City's broadest paved thoroughfare.

Notably, too, the song's publisher was the Lambeth Music Company, then located on Mulberry Street, in Syracuse. The company is known to have notated and published the compositions of several local songsters, including the instant *Dr. R. E. Reynard.* Contemporary newspaper accounts attest that this local *juris doctorate* and amateur parlor banjoist was an inveterate letter-writer and editorialist in the city's newspapers, oft inveighing against the impending interment of the Erie Canal. A practicing attorney, and not without means, Reynard may indeed have underwritten the publication of his broadside ballad lamenting the passing of the era of the Erie Canal. But by the early 1920's, the halcyon days of the Erie Canal were already over, and the waterway was broadly impugned by elected and appointed municipal officials as an "open sewer, stagnant & fetid & noxious." Also soon to pass was the once prosperous Lambeth Music Company, itself, when sheet music sales were eclipsed by the novelty of simply listening to wax cylinders and shellac discs, neither of which required the expertise and labor of amateur parlor pianists making music in the home. Thus, the *Erie Canal Song* could have been published no later than 1929, when the Lambeth Music Company folded.

Recent archival research has turned up only a single instance of a direct descendant of Dr. R. E. Reynard performing the song himself, accompanied by banjo and guitar, remarkably preserved in almost pristine condition on a contemporaneously made recording.

Erie Canal Song

Well, me and my friend, my friend Sal
We went down to that Erie Canal;
Roamed them paths where the mules once walked
Haulin' plank barges from lock to lock

All the way from Albany to Buffalo,
From the Hudson River to Ontario:

> *Low bridge, everybody down*
> *Low bridge, 'cause we're comin' to a town.*

Well, I kicked a can, and Sal hummed a tune
While we walked for a stretch
'Neath the full autumn moon;
And Sal got to talkin', and he said to me
Somethin' that he first heard
On his grandfather's knee:

"They dug straight 'cross the state
Layin' limestone walls
All along that Erie Canal."   Singin':

> *Oh, low bridge, everybody down*
> *Low bridge, 'cause we're comin' to a town.*

Well, Rome wasn't built, and Syracuse
Was nothing but a swamp
Till the Canal come through.
In its halcyon days
There was none that hadn't heard,
And there was some that even called it
A "Wonder of the World."

There was towns and bars and white hotels
All along that Erie Canal

Oh, low bridge, everybody down
Oh, low bridge, 'cause we're comin' to a town.

Well, the towns got bigger
And the cities grew
Where there once was only woods,
Till the Canal come through.
And the bridges got lower
And the paths got paved,
And the traffic got fast
When the motorcar came

And the businessmen said,
"The canal's seen its day,"
And the newspapers wrote
How the canal was "in the way —"

Oh, low bridge, everybody down
Oh low bridge, 'cause we're comin' to a town.

Well, me and my friend, my friend Sal
Oh, we went down to that Erie Canal,
And Sal sort of whispered
While we looked about:
"It was nothin' but a grave
With the ends knocked out."

And we sat on the curb,
And we watched the cars
Goin' a mile a minute
Down Erie Boulevard.

Oh, low bridge, everybody down
Oh, low bridge,
'Cause we're comin' to a town.

Oh, low bridge, everybody down,
Oh, low bridge,
Cause we're comin' to a town.

Slave Wages

Nickel City Medicine Show

If the Erie Canal was the route by which commerce and the industry would arrive in the wilds of upstate New York, it was also the thoroughfare for the theatrical and musical talent that would migrate from the already crowded cities of the eastern seaboard and alight in the emerging frontier towns along the new waterway. The Nickel City Medicine Show was just one of the many now forgotten troupes that "went on the road" by taking to the canal, leaving a legacy of music halls, opera houses and theatres in their wake.

Touring the canal towns as a *medicine* show, the company would defy the almost irresistible financial temptation after the Civil War to bill itself as a blackface *minstrel* show. Remembered today in shame and regarded with scorn, both white and black entertainers would "black up" with burnt cork, adopting the exaggerated makeup and mannerisms of the plantation "darkie" in ostensibly comical monologues and musical skits – a misbegotten genre that became the most popular form of entertainment of the age and, sadly, remained wildly popular until well into the mid-twentieth century. Notably, the performers of the Nickel City Medicine Show were never to "black up." Instead – and almost certainly as a political statement — they performed exclusively in *whiteface*.

The Nickel City Medicine Show was also unusual in at least one other significant respect: while little else is known about the company, it is now beyond question that both Irving Washington *(Smith)* and Melvin Herman *(Jones),* the troupe's two leading players, and the vocalists on the instant recording, were card-carrying members of the IWW, or *Wobblies.* The IWW was an international union of labor agitators who were regarded with notoriety as *Reds* by even the then-leftist mainstream American labor movement. There is no extant explanation as to why *Slave Wages* was not included in *The Little Red Songbook,* the IWW's now-famous song manifesto, but the omission must have been a sharp disappointment to the troupe.

Nevertheless, the results of Nickel City's collaboration were indeed subversive, as is evidenced by the rare recorded sample of the repartee between Washington and Herman which prefaces their pro-labor lament, *Slave Wages.* This novelty song is doubly remarkable for encompassing the running time of *two* Edison wax cylinders, here seamlessly edited into a single selection for the *ANTHOLOGY OF NEW YORK FOLK MUSIC.*

Spoken Introduction

JONES: Good evening, Mister Smith.

SMITH: And likewise, Mister Jones.

JONES: Let's do a *work* song, Mister Smith.

Prologue to violin and banjo, recitativo:

SMITH: In Adam's fall sinned we all
                   And get bread now by sweat of brow

JONES: In Eve's travail we're born a'wail
                   And women's work is "cook and sew."

SMITH: And *that* was the first division of *labor!*

Sung, in forlorn unison:

Slave Wages

You can dig the black hole
of Calcutta
You can build up
the great pyramids

You can weed every garden
in Babylonia
You can paper the Great Wall
of China

You can lift & move the rocks
of the ages,
All they'll ever pay you
is slave wages.

You can work all your life on the railroad,
You can work off your years on the farm
You can clerk in a house counting paper & gold,
You can soldier a post, called to arms

You can turn the Black Forest
to white pages,
All they'll ever pay you
is slave wages.

Spoken:

MR. SMITH: Now, I've got one, Mister Jones,
                    That's a riddle *and* a fable:

                    How long did Cain hate his brother?

MR. JONES: For as long as he was Abel!

Sung:

You can etch gentle lambs & wild lions,
You can paint the starr'd night over Arles,
You can spin at a wheel under Britain,
You can hang on a tree over Zion

You can go down
with the saviors & sages,
All they'll ever give you
is slave wages.

All they'll ever pay you is slave wages.

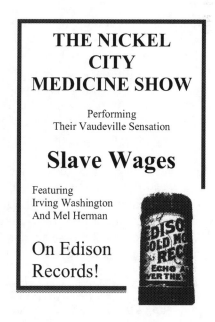

Broadside/
Rural Blues/
Murder Ballad?
circa 1914

[Artists Anonymous] †

Ballads about schoolhouse fires were all the rage in the upstate New York of the roaring twenties, and no collection of vintage New York State folk music would be complete without at least one exemplar of the genre, which enjoyed broad popularity in the early decades of recorded song. The typical penchant for auditory novelty sound effects, as evident in so many early sound recordings, is prominent here, with the violin and howling vocals, and even the bending of the banjo notes, approximating the wailings of little children perishing in the blaze.

Preserved only on a single unlabeled wax cylinder, fortuitously discovered in the rafters of a New Hampshire dairy barn in 2011 just minutes before its razing, nothing is known of the provenance of the recording. A three-piece ensemble seems to be in evidence (assuming the banjoist is doubling on the harmonica), but musicologists and folklorists have been unable to identify a likely performing artist or string-band of the period.

† Professional (and aspiring) musical archaeologists are invited to forward any unearthed information regarding the artist, date, place and circumstances of this recording to CARDIFF HISTORICAL RECORDINGS, with appropriate artist credit and contributor acknowledgement to be included in future editions of this issue.

The Brookfield Schoolhouse Fire

In a village once called Brookfield
In the year nineteen-aught-five
'Twas was a terrible schoolhouse fire
Not one soul got out alive

From the littlest of children
To the uppermost of grades
All 47 perished
In the Brookfield schoolhouse blaze.

In the foothills of the Catskills
By a brook that farm-town lay
And the children came from miles around
To their school that fateful day.

No one knows how it started
Though the sheriff was to say
That the coal furnace exploded
While the collier was away.

But yonder on the hillside
Standing underneath the trees
Watched the boy who played with matches
Whom the other children teased.

This sad tale is a story
That we should remember well
But nobody knows the story, for
There was no child to tell

No child survived to tell the tale
And pass the story down
So, in a vale out in the Catskill hills,
Is the ghost of that lost town.

Thanksgiving Day Blues

Blind Reuben Pascal

Born of uncertain parentage, and with congenital syphilis, and hence hare-lipped and sightless, Blind Reuben Pascal was abandoned as an infant on the doorstep of the Erie County Home for the Colored Blind. There he spent his childhood acquiring a facility at his fingertips with the (then) recently popularized Braille alphabet, as well as – fortuitously, for the incipience of upstate New York's rural blues music – the fretboard of a cheap Sears® guitar.

That it would be a *guitar* – given out to little Blind Reuben by the orphanage concertmaster, Leonard Porter – was unusual for the time, in that bandmasters at colored orphanages customarily outfitted their charges with brass instruments, prominently cornets. But Porter likely recognized that the hare-lipped Pascal would never be able to accomplish the embouchure required of a horn player, and the blind child's lifelong idiosyncratic sense of rhythm must have quickly disqualified him as a drummer. At seven years old, Blind Reuben Pascal was thus assigned and entrusted with a catgut strung guitar. The rest was history, and would become the stuff of myth. For Little Blind Reuben would come to be known as The King of the Upstate New York Blues Singers, a legendary figure, made perhaps more enigmatic by his lifelong refusal to be photographed.

Similarly mysterious, until understood, is Blind Reuben's refusal to play the guitar unless outfitted in a pair of heavy asbestos welder's gloves, thereby imparting the characteristic and unique muffled sound that has since been copied by legions of aspiring blues guitarists. However, as explained by his sometime performing partner, the banjoist Odell Jackson (not featured on his recording), Pascal's signature style was less a matter of deliberate technique or quixotic affectation than a necessity for the blind performer. According to Jackson's autobiography, *Bluesmen as I Knew 'Em,* Blind Reuben was a voracious reader, and reportedly feared that the obduration of his fingertips caused by the guitar strings would render him unable to scan Braille.

Odell Jackson's blues memoir is, of course, noteworthy for one further – and stunning – revelation regarding the mysterious rural blues guitarist: although abandoned on the doorstep of the Erie County Home for the Colored Blind, Reuben Pascal was actually, in all probability, a *white* child. Jackson's observation that "Though duskily complected, it is my opinion that Blind Reuben was a Caucasian person" cannot be confirmed by any known portrait of the bluesman: only one extant photograph, perhaps apocryphal, reveals a gloved guitarist facing the corner of the bathtub in the Rochester, New York, hotel room where he cut his now historic twelve sides for the Irondequoit Furniture Company.

If indeed a "Caucasian person" as averred by Jackson, Blind Reuben Pascal's achievement as Upstate New York's most famous exemplar of the African American indigenous art form of the blues is an astonishing example of Nurture over Nature, and a testament to the transformative power of such music.

The only known photograph of Blind Reuben Pascal, "King of the Upstate New York Blues Singers." This promotional picture, taken surreptitiously during Blind Reuben's only known recording session in 1934, depicts the artist wearing his trademark welder's gloves and performing in a bathtub, presumably for acoustical purposes. Later aspiring blues guitarists would adopt these methods in attempts to 'find' Pascal's sound, but none would ever replicate it. Photo authenticated by Odell Jackson, courtesy of Irondequoit Records Archive, Irondequoit, N.Y.

Thanksgiving Day Blues

It was the fourth Wednesday in November,
I was struttin' in the dirt;
Had first place in the pecking order,
I was just a bold young Turk.

> I didn't know
> The price I'd pay:
> When your oat sowin' days are over,
> You still gotta work Thanksgiving Day.

Well, I clucked and I hissed at the farmer
Till he entered the livestock yard;
It was then that I saw the big cleaver
— I started runnin' hard!

> It was my worst nightmare
> come true:
> That farmer was havin' me over for dinner,
> And he looked just like Fred Perdue.

Now, the farmer was talkin' turkey,
He was showin' who ruled the roost
When he grabbed at my neck and he caught me,
He was out to cook my goose!

> Why does it have
> to be this way?
> You can sit on the platter of honor,
> But you gotta work Thanksgiving Day.

Well, I was caught with my neck on a tree stump,
And I couldn't lay any fast golden eggs;
So I fought till I heard a quick swish and a thump
— It was then that I lost my head!

    I saw a turkey,
    a decapitee —
    Make a dash for the fence, take a long running jump,
    Then it headed down the highway free! (Without me.)

Now, they'll get you fat, sassy, and happy
And there's always all kinds of chicks,
But when it's time that you want to retire
You don't get no benefits!

    And it's a goddamned
    Awful shame —
    You'll never get put out to pasture,
    'Cause you've gotta work Thanksgiving Day.

So whether you're scratchin' a barnyard
Or force-fed mash in some tiny cage,
Remember, young Turk, it ain't over
Till you go to work
Thanksgiving Day.

Vintage ticket and show poster, in pristine condition. Courtesy of
West Cardiff University special collections, used by permission. Circa 1940.

Decapitated Donna

Credited to "Coleman-Spates Shows"
Performing Artist(s) unknown.

> *Carnival Ballad/*
> *Novelty Tune/*
> *Murder Ballad*
> *1941*

Remarkably early on, the novelty of recorded sound was almost immediately employed to present *special effects* that might heighten a sung narrative, as evidenced by this melodramatic ballad about a rube's after-hours encounter with a tragic sideshow act, DECAPITATED DONNA.

Credited on the record label to the "Coleman-Spates Shows" – a carnival midway organization that hired out to upstate New York's county fairs and firemen's field days during the summer months of the 1930's – the only existing (one-sided) 78 rpm shellac disc that sources this recording was likely sold as a souvenir outside the freak-show to the carnival marks as they were exiting the tent. The identity of the balladeer, gravel-voiced but oddly operatic, has not conclusively been proven, although University of West Cardiff ethnomusicologist and acoustician Lazlo Horvath has persuasively matched digitalized voice-prints of this 1941 recording with the isolated vocal from OLD MAID, a 45 rpm single released in 1962 by the short-lived Tanager Records. Per the Tanager label, OLD MAID's authorship and solo performance were attributed to Jabez Dodge, possibly the same former medicine show songster billed by that name in a 1916 show poster. *See,* OLD MAID, *infra.*

Dodge's putative performance of DECAPITATED DONNA must, at this time, remain conjectural, but the singer's primary influence is obvious: the growling, gut-bucket vocal has drawn comparisons by more than one critic to the 1930's vocalizations of Louis Armstrong. In turn, the influence of this recording upon the song stylizations of Tom Waits, some three generations later and albeit (to date) unacknowledged by Waits himself, is unmistakable.

ADMIT ONE

COLEMAN-SPATES SIDESHOWS
25¢   DECAPITATED DONNA   25¢

Decapitated Donna

'Twas after midnight at the end of the midway,
On the last night of the New York State Fair;
I was walking through the sideshow poster alley,
I saw a painted lady there —

> She was pictured with a carwreck in the background:
> A bloodtorn dress, and broken glass was everywhere;
> She held her severed head as if it was a lantern
> — Her head was hanging by the hair.

> I gave the fat man in the ticket cage a quarter
> To see the truth, or maybe just take up the dare;
> There was a dusty velvet rope and I stepped over,
> As the crash of metal through a bullhorn blared:

>> *New Year's Eve one winter*
>> *Years have come and gone;*
>> *Donna waited for her date to take her*
>> *To the junior class prom.*

>> *He pinned the corsage on her*
>> *Red roses and her long white gown;*
>> *They drank the wine but didn't touch their dinner*
>> *— She would never come home.*

>> *It was a cold and lonely moonlit winter's night;*
>> *She wouldn't live to see the light.*
>> *There's something lost she has to make up for —*
>> *She won't be dancing anymore.*

> In the musty canvas darkness I could see her,
> Electric candlelight, and I tried not to stare:
> There was a stump under the scarf over her shoulders,
> She was just sitting, knitting something in a chair

> She wore a yellowed formal gown, bloodstained and tattered
> The rose corsage was dead, her broken heels were charred;
> And on the table in the candlelight beside her
> — What looked like a woman's head was in a jar.

She kept on rocking for a quarter of an hour,
While I waited, but she did not seem aware;
And I watched her knit a little yellow sweater
'Til the lights dimmed, and I had to leave her there.

> *The car stopped for the crossroads, and she kissed him;*
> *They didn't see the red light change to green —*
> *They never noticed, — 'Never knew what hit them' —*
> *The coroner said later at the scene.*

> *The road was icy, and the truck too fast;*
> *The car smashed through a roadside shed —*
> *A roughcut board, like buckshot broke the glass —*
> *And little Donna lost her head.*

Well, I've always been drawn in by any victim,
It's an attraction for the tragic circumstance;
And Decapitated Donna was no exception,
So I went around to wait behind the tents

When the shows closed I stayed low between the trailers,
'Til I saw her slow approach, some kind of hunchback;
With her head crooked and low between her shoulders —
And I knew then, Donna had been born like that.

The affliction that she lived with wasn't pretty
There wasn't anything to say, I just felt sorry
And the last thing that she needed was my pity
So I left her with her knitting and her story.

> *Have a good night, Donna*
> *Count the two-headed sheep,*
> *The hundred pound iguana*
> *Can maybe curl up at your feet;*

> *And maybe the Human Pin-Cushion's your husband*
> *And the fat lady just really likes to eat —*
> *Maybe you're tired of the boys*
>   *who want to join the circus*
> *And you wish we'd all go home*
>   *and let you sleep.*

Aisle of the Waters

Patricia Ryder

Erie Canal Song/
Murder Ballad
1949

The only "field recording" to be included on the *ANTHOLOGY, Aisle of the Waters* is also the only selection to appear without accompanying artwork, for none exists. Replete with the economy of line so typical of the rural story-song, any illustration of the tale and its two tragic personages would have to be gestetically etched in stray charcoal marks, scratched and slashed, this way and that, into a rude and evocative portraiture. Recorded on primitive equipment in a turnpike motel outside of Waterville, New York, this completely improvised field recording (both lyric & music) is credited to its only known participant, upstate blues guitarist Patricia Ryder.

Aisle of the Waters

There's an aisle
There's an aisle
Far out on the western miles;
There's an aisle
There's an aisle
They call it the Aisle of the Waters.

Well, I went down there
To a tavern
I hit the tables 'til the glasses danced.
Yes, I went down there
To a tavern
I hit the tables until the glasses danced

Then I looked out of the window
She was coming with her blonde hair flying
Was running
Was running
By the Aisle of the Waters.

I stood up, and walked across
I was there at the doorway waiting
When she came in, and she stood there
Like she was at a lake, and watching skaters skating

And I wondered, yes, yes, yes, I wondered
I wondered if tonight we might be walking
By the banks, those dark banks
Of the Aisle of the Waters.

Well, the banks they were shady
We went walking in the moonlight, I thought maybe
That someday, we might stray, we might take that final walk
Down to the altar

Walking down beneath the shady banks
To the Aisle of the Waters.

Oh, mother
Don't you cry for me,
Oh, mother, don't you weep;
Your tears
They wet my grave shroud
And now I cannot sleep

For I took her
Out and walking
By the Aisle of the Waters—

And tomorrow
My dear mother

I will marry the ropemaker's daughter.

Volunteer Fireman's Waltz
Seven Years

Barndance Waltzes/
Reels & Jigs/
Rural Blues
1952

/ Blue Wedding Dress

Onan Jones's One-Man-Band

In 1951, an aspiring 19-year-old fiddle and banjo player who had never before ventured beyond the environs of his hometown of Bristol, Tennessee, climbed aboard a passenger car of the Norfolk-Southern railroad with a carpetbag full of clothes and his two instruments in tow, heading *north,* with the audacious aspiration of bringing his singular country string-band sound to what jazz musicians had for more than two decades been calling the *Big Apple* – New York City.

Onan Jones – reputedly so named when his fundamentalist but illiterate father cracked open the first pages of the family bible and stabbed his index finger into the text of Genesis – was only six years old when the legendary talent scout Ralph Peer arrived in town with state-of-the-art electronic recording equipment and a well-publicized open invitation to the "hillbilly acts" of the region to audition for the Victor label. The ensuing 1926 "Bristol Sessions" would put Onan Jones's hometown on the map as the place where such seminal and eminent artists as The Carter Family, Jimmie Rodgers, Eck Dunford, and Ernest Stoneham were discovered – a proud history of which the budding string musician was almost certainly aware. But by the late 1940's, it must have been equally apparent to the youngster that neither Peer nor any other producer would be returning to Bristol to scout out the next generation of talent, and that if young Onan were to find his fame and fortune, he would have to journey to where the recording studios were now permanently located – in New York City.

And, indeed, the Big Apple could well have become New York State's capitol city of country string-band music — just as it had been a mecca for jazz in the 1920's, and would (a scant decade later) become the birthplace of the folk revival of the early '60's – had not the adolescent Onan Jones solitarily imbibed in at least one too many (and possibly more) celebratory jar(s) of white moonshine upon his first time crossing Tennessee's Sullivan County line, thereby falling into a dead slumber on the train. He would thence deeply sleep through Kentucky, West Virginia, and New Jersey, and, unconscious when the train stopped at his original destination of New York City, was to eventually awaken somewhere north of Albany with what he would describe, in a press interview conducted long after the fact, as "the most down-bust, emptied-out, brain-killer-pain and crippling-pure-aching hangover that anybody must of [sic] ever lived through." But he would live to drink again, and Utica, New York – where Onan Jones ultimately disembarked the train – was now by chance destined to host Upstate New York's solo progenitor of country string-band music.

Young Onan would take to the Utica streets as a lone busker, and by temperament and inclination, would ever after remain a solo performer. The stories are legion of his innate inability to make music with anyone else, beginning with the abandoned 1951 sessions produced by Utica disc jockey George "Bud" Garland. "I found the kid on the street, thought he had his own unique sound, so I decided to record him," Bud Garland recalled in a 1974 interview, "and I put him in with the best string bands I could find. Three good local country-type bands, one after another. It just didn't work. By himself, he could just whack 'em out. But put anybody with him, he couldn't keep time, froze up, was just terrible. And that was before he started in drinking. He drank alone – always on the sly – I never actually saw the kid take a drink, but he would come back from the head into the studio reeking of booze, and then he'd get ornery, insulting the other musicians, until nobody wanted anything to do with him." The tapes of these initial sessions were, evidently, wiped.

But Bud Garland persisted. If Jones's antisocial approach to music-making and his unsociable drinking made musical collaboration impossible, it did tend to improve the youth's own performance, Garland had noticed, and Jones was an adept multi-instrumentalist. Eight months after the abortive 1951 session, Garland conceived of how Onan Jones might be successfully recorded. Inspired by the similarly ornery Sidney Bechet's 1941 experimental and pioneering multi-track recording of all six instrumental parts of *The Sheik of Araby* (tenor and soprano sax, clarinet, piano, bass and drums, successively recorded on a 78 rpm acetate), Garland decided to attempt a second session, with his artist quadruple-tracking himself on vocal and banjo, violin, guitar, and upright bass. But, knowing full well that Onan Jones was no Sidney Bechet, Garland also hit upon a stratagem which he thought "might cover a multitude of musical sins" – recording the young artist's successive masters at the somewhat novelty speed of 16 and 2/3 revolutions per minute.

Today's elder audiophiles may still recall that the phonographic turntables of their childhoods were likely equipped with a knob or lever that not only alternated between the now standardized 45 and 33 and 1/3 speeds, as well as the now (lamentably) obsolesced 78 rpm setting, but also included a mysterious *fourth* speed, 16 and 2/3 rpm. Children might switch to this obscure setting to sample the novelty effect of retarding a standard rpm record so as to make the performer sound drunken and dense (a practice which, incidentally, ruined the grooves of 45's and LP's, and accounts for the extreme scarcity of mint condition Alvin and the Chipmunks releases in the collectors' market) – but *music* records actually released in the 16 and 2/3 rpm format would always be a rarity. Because a standard 12" platter could include up to two hours of content at 16 and 2/3 rpm, the format was primarily developed to market "talking books" to the blind, and for instructional recordings accompanying filmstrips that were typically punctuated by *beeps* to cue the projector operator to change the frame. However, the lugubrious speed was of such low fidelity that few solely musical records were produced in the format – until the 1950's.

For reasons not readily explicable, the 1950's saw a brief flourishing of experimentation in the format, as evidenced by the 1954 *Prestige* pressing of Miles Davis's *Modern Jazz Giants,* a now much-prized collector's curio of the era. Other companies were already producing extended song collections to be played as "background" music in restaurants and hotel lobbies, where the lo-fi quality of the sound reproduction was regarded as acceptable, in view of the advantage of having a waiter or desk clerk attend to the flipping of the platter at mere one-hour intervals. And, curiously, the musical genre which would see the greatest (albeit brief) upsurge in the format was what we would now call "Country and Western", or white rural music. Thus, what Bud Garland would boast of in 1974 as his "whizz-bang" idea of recording solo string-band artist Onan Jones at 16 and 2/3 rpm was hardly revolutionary by 1951; moreover, the decelerated method had the incalculable advantage of enabling Garland to record Jones's successive takes of vocal and solo instrumental iterations without obvious discordances.

When records are genuinely appreciated as precious cultural artifacts, rather than hoarded as collectible fetish objects, the 16 and 2/3 multi-tracking of Jones's forlorn string-band songs are, indubitably, a consummate exemplar of the medium befitting the message. For Onan Jones was a lone balladeer, solitary and singular, innately unable to create music in the company of other musicians, thus necessitating his insular approach to recording. The lyrics of these songs concomitantly provide a portrait of the introverted artist making a play (likely unsuccessful) for a girl who has come to a town's annual Fireman's Field Days with her date *(Volunteer Fireman's Waltz,* a paean to Central New York's rural town carnival fundraisers for its local fire departments, which traditionally featured open-air string bands and dancing, as well as Ferris wheels and kids' rides and fireworks) and a singer so cursed by bad luck that he is marking seven years of celibacy *(Seven Years).* But the most telling of these compositions is the flip-side of the disc, *Blue Wedding Dress.* The first locally produced string-band side to become a regional hit song, and even today a standard oft performed by Central New York's country, bluegrass, and string ensembles, *Blue Wedding Dress* relates the sad tale of its narrator misfortunately wed, and then left to "quietly get off" beside his dead- drunk and sluttish bride. The double entendre, daring for 1952, was not lost on local radio listeners and record buyers. Nor would there be any listener complaints about the relatively brief duration of Onan Jones's only official release. Recorded at 16 and 2/3 rpm, this ten-inch, two-inch center hole record could have included an additional thirty to forty minutes of music.

But it was enough.

GARLAND RECORDS

4:12
16 ⅔
rpm

BLUE WEDDING DRESS
ONAN JONES

Volunteer Fireman's Waltz

1. Without sayin' a word,
   We was waltzin';
   The big band was playin'
   And watchin' —

   Your old man was standin'
   On the sidelines,
   And hard up against you
   I tried lines:

   Money talks, money breaks
   Money makes some mistakes —
   An' he's payin'
   for both of our drinks.

   But it isn't my fault
   If you asked me to waltz —
   An' you're bringin' me
       up to the brink.

2. Now the candle, it's burnin'
   At both ends;
   We're dancin', pretendin'
   We're just friends —

   But now as the hour
   Draws near,
   Won't you bend your blond head,
   Lend an ear:

   Money talks, money breaks
   Money makes some mistakes —
   But I can't say
   it's anyone's fault

   You were dancin' so near
   That I fell for you, dear,
   While the band played
       the Tennessee Waltz

3.

— That beautiful Tennesee Waltz —

Yes, the band played that Tennessee Waltz.

Seven Years

Seven years, the mirror's been broken
Seven years, the hat's been on the bed
Seven years since the curse was first spoken
Seven years since a blessing's been said.

Seven years since you first met me,
Seven years since you last left me,
Seven years is a long time to wait —
I should leave you, but I'm seven years late.

Seven years since the ladder's been passed under
Seven years since that black cat crossed my path
Seven years since the lightning and the thunder
Struck twice in the same place — with all its wrath!

Well, the Congress says, "Prosperity
Is just around the corner,"
And the President, he promises me
That things are looking better;

But the rich are getting richer,
And the poor keep getting poorer
— And I don't think you'll ever get straight —

Seven years, and I'm seven years late;

Seven years is a long time to wait.

Blue Wedding Dress

Her daddy had the shotgun
Her mama baked the cake
Sent sister Susie to the garden
To pick a big bouquet

Then they put me in a green room
With a suit that had a vest
I couldn't look while she was putting on
Her BLUE WEDDING DRESS.

Well, the preacher came to see me
While I clipped the bow-tie on
Like he'd visit a shoplifter
Condemned to die at dawn

The maid of honor was a rounder
And the best man was depressed
But the bride was in her glory
In her BLUE WEDDING DRESS.

When I heard the words "Do you sir,
For better or for worse
Take this woman wed forever?"
She whispered "Dear, I swear it's yours"

I didn't want to face her daddy
Or to disappoint the guests
So in two minutes she was married
In her   BLUE WEDDING DRESS.

We had a hell of a reception
And the jokes flowed like the beer
'Bout how she had one in the oven
And her time was drawin' near

She drank and danced with all the boys there
Some who'd seen her in much less
Than just the garter tossed from under
her BLUE WEDDING DRESS.

(SPOKEN:)

    Now, the broken bedsprings buckle
    With every racking cough
    She is sleeping still beside me
    As I quietly get off

    And I listen to her breathing
    And I smell her whiskey breath
    But even as I'm leaving
    My heart's already left.

(SUNG:)

But I lay down for one last time
Put my head against her breast
And I feel the lace and satin
Of her BLUE WEDDING DRESS.

Yes I lay down for one last time
Put my head against her breast
And I feel the lace and satin
Of her BLUE WEDDING DRESS.

Machine Chantey / Roadside Motel

Rural Blues /
Work Songs
1934

Blind Reuben Pascal

Were it not for the controversy occasioned by recent forensic analysis of Blind Reuben Pascal's *Machine Chantey* and *Roadside Motel,* these 1934 performances would appear earlier in the *ANTHOLOGY*'s otherwise roughly chronological presentation of the folk and blues music of Upstate New York. But that analysis, conducted by University of West Cardiff ethnomusicologist and acoustician Lazlo Horvath, is now generally accepted to have conclusively proven that the catgut strings of Blind Reuben's guitar could not possibly have produced the piecing timbre so evident on the original recordings.[3] Thus, for over eighty years, roots music aficionados have been deprived of authentic renditions of two of the seminal recorded performances of Buffalo's most revered bluesman.

The likely explanation lies in the primitive recording methods of the Irondequoit Furniture Company, which ventured into record production only as an adjunct to selling its line of phonograph cabinets. The shellac 78 rpm platters were principally demonstration records, made to exhibit the lifelike dynamic range of the then-state-of-the-art science of modern sound reproduction, and so to then sell the cabinetry for their trumpet-horn-flowered phonographs. *Thanksgiving Day Blues,* Pascal's primeval and now legendary record, although cut in the same session, must have been deemed *dynamic* enough. But for *Roadside Motel* and *Machine Chantey,* more percussive sides, with Pascal predominately thumping and slapping and knocking his guitar between catgut guitar licks, some acoustical juicing was evidently deemed necessary. The (unknown) 1934 sound engineer on the session employed one of the few recording tricks then available to alter recorded sound – slowing down the rotation of the platter being cut during actual recording – so as to enervate the listener's experience of an intensified and heightened performance when the pressed record was re-played at standard speed – and to thereby to sell more phonograph cabinets.

It is hard, now, to quibble with that commercial, if not virtuously authentic, decision. The Irondequoit Furniture Company would go on to sell some 72,465 phonographic

---

[3] Horvath has noted that the discrepancy between *Machine* Chantey's actual running time of 3:03 and the label-listed duration of 3:27 offered the first clue that something was amiss about these two widely celebrated recordings. After digitized analysis ruled out any possibility of an edit, Horvath slowed the recording and thereby rediscovered the song as originally performed by Blind Reuben. *Roadside Motel* was, then, similarly restored.

cabinets between 1932 and 1937, in the depths of the Great Depression, and would not declare bankruptcy until the eve of the Second World War. By that time, sadly, Blind Reuben Pascal was a long-forgotten blues troubadour, having eked out a living for the remainder of his life by plucking out chards from popular song piano rolls with his Braille stylus.

But Pascal would be rescued from obscurity – albeit posthumously – upon the resurgence of interest in American "roots" music during the "folk revival" of the 1950's and early 60's, when a new generation of enthusiasts took to the backroads of such musically fecund landscapes as Mississippi and North Carolina in search of the possibly still-living bluesmen whom they had heard on the already antique 78 rpm shellac discs that circulated among collectors. A few of these protean bluesmen, such as Skip James and Mississippi John Hurt, were actually thus rediscovered, and were recruited late in their lives to headline folk festivals and cut new records for the briefly burgeoning market in roots music.

Upstate New Yorker Pascal, who passed in 1954, was unfortunately not among them. But the 1962 rediscovery of twelve 1930's sides recorded for Irondequoit, including the sides presented herein, would ultimately assure Blind Reuben's place in the canon. Now re-engineered to restore their original running times, as performed, the *ANTHOLOGY* for the first time presents the definitive versions of Blind Reuben Pascal's *Machine Chantey* and *Roadside Motel.*

Machine Chantey

Screeching like a stuck hog
Into a black lunch box,
Suction pump is choking with a sneeze

Howling like a scowdog
Not even nine o'clock –
Is that the way you want your face to freeze?

    Well, pickle my knuckles in vinegar
    And saw up my shins into chops,
    Then cut out my heart with a bindery knife
    Paint my ribs red with barbecue sauce –

    Flay off my skin and deep fry it to rinds
    And hang me on hooks by the heels,
    Chop my guts into sausage, grind my bones into lime
    But you can't make a buck on the squeal.

Buy off all of the riff-raff,
Lower 'em into a mine shaft
With a guilded cage crammed full of dead canaries.

Don't want to wake the neighbors,
Landlord's buried under the floorboards,
So oil that water, fill those gears with grease!

    And it's many the midnight ride, boys
    And there's many have ridden the waves,
    And there's many gone over the side, boys
    And perished in watery graves

    So pickle my knuckles in vinegar
    And hang me on hooks by the heels,
    Then cut out my heart with a bindery knife
    – But you can't make a buck on the squeal.

Roadside Motel

Screams in the heat of a late August night,
A few rooms down the row
Somebody's fighting, somebody pulls a knife,
Smashes out the window—

There was three people livin' in one little room,
Now there's none, since the big old man fell
And two brothers went handcuffed in the state trooper's car
From this roadside motel.

Well, it's forty-five dollars a week, in advance
And it's forty-five, security
So for just ninety bucks, it aint hard to get in,
It aint easy to leave—

Everybody needs someplace to legally sleep,
Everybody needs somewhere to dwell
But there's nowhere to go
When the rents are so steep
Everywhere but this roadside motel.

You can hear conversations
Through paper-thin walls,
Where a fam'ly may be crowded in—
And the hotplates are blowin' out fuses,
 'Cause we're all
Cookin' dinners in tins—

Mama feeds liquor to three little kids,
It shuts 'em up when they start in to yell—
She's got blankets in the shower stall
For one of 'em's crib

In this roadside motel.

Old Maid

Carnival Ballad
1962

Jabez Dodge

That this odd, plaintive carnival ballad is credited on the label of the 45 rpm A-side of the Tanager Records' release to "Jabez Dodge" raises intriguing possibilities, for there is no documentary evidence (at least, since 1806) of any person by that name, save for a vintage 1916 medicine show poster billing *Jabez Dodge* as a "featured attraction." Assuming that such an attraction would have been then at least in his twenties, Dodge must have been quite elderly by the time of this 1962 recording. And, if University of West Cardiff ethnomusicologist and acoustician Lazlo Horvath is correct in his surmise that Dodge was the uncredited performer of the seminal carnival ballad DECAPITATED DONNA in 1941, we begin to be able to sketch a bare-bones biography of a fascinating songster who began his career as a medicine show performer, was decades later employed in some capacity as a carnival worker, and finally, somehow, waxed a critically significant platter with a swiftly waning record company in the formative early sixties.

We want to know more. Typically, such historical research might begin with a delving into the archives of Dodge's record company, but no such company files are, apparently, extant. Tanager Records, evidently a fly-by-night record company operating out of Binghamton, New York, in 1962 incorporated itself under one of the few avian names not (even then) already taken by other record companies. Tanager's only four other discoverable released singles – all of them antic polkas by "Jerry Wierszalin and his Polka Troubadors" – do not remotely resemble the stately and haunting OLD MAID, although the B-side of that single (omitted herein) comprises an uncredited and almost unlistenable see-saw calliope instrumental with accordion and clarinet accompaniment, possibly a collaborative effort by keyboardist Dodge accompanied by the Polka Troubadors. But we simply do not know, and so cannot, for certain, say. Was young Dodge's 1916 *entre* into show business interrupted by service in the First World War? Very possibly, although no enlistee nomenclated as *Jabez Dodge* appears in the searchable annals of the (then named) Department of War. And if, indeed, Dodge had at last clawed out of obscurity to belatedly grasp at the cusp of popularity with DECAPITATED DONNA (albeit uncredited) in 1941, did the subsequent ASCAP recording ban in the early 1940's dash any prospect that he might, at last, achieve commercial recognition? And is it not tragically ironic that Dodge's last bid to have his music finally heard should be cut with a Binghamton record company doomed by its A&R department's apparent penchant for polkas?

Yes. In all probability. For despite the inexplicable gaps in his more than half-century career, the conclusion follows that Jabez Dodge was, at 20-year intervals, a three-time loser. Despite this record's persisting inclusion on Binghamton jukeboxes (see below), it is impossible to argue, in strictly nation-wide commercial terms, otherwise. And yet, such a career compasses the known recorded history of the folk and blues music of upstate New York, and it is thus beyond cavil that Dodge deserves a place in our pantheon of the region's truly greatest balladeers and songsters. That his canonical status rests upon the audio documentation of only two commercially released carnival ballads – his (arguably putative) DECAPITATED DONNA and Tanager's OLD MAID – is unsurprising, given that the unsurpassed literary and melodic quality of these two recorded compositions, and the supremely evocative performances given them by Dodge therein, can only be regarded as *transcendent*. We would do well to remember that Herman Melville left us only one great novel, and T.S. Elliot, a single great poem. Likewise, in the cut-throat 20th Century music business, with cardboard-sleeved LP's and jewel-cased CD artifacts glutting record store bins (before those stores went bankrupt and out of business), certain 'one-hit-wonders' indeed attained classic status, and even today commercially survive as viable down-loads and as classic-format radio playlist standards. And, so, it follows that a truly great artist, striving to stand kneecap-deep against the undertow tide of the fashions of recorded music, need only leave one single immortal work of art to be remembered, and eternally revered, at least for as long as human eternity may last. Submitted for critical and lay listener consideration, then, is a motive thesis of ANTHOLOGY OF NEW YORK STATE FOLK MUSIC: that Jabez Dodge is one such consummate artist, and worthy of remembrance.

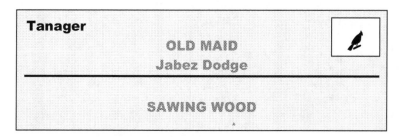

Old Maid

She was standin' all alone
Out on them carnival grounds,
It was late
The stars were shining through the cold

And the painted dancin' ponies
On that merry-go-round
Had stopped spinning,
And the Ferris wheel had slowed.

They were shuttin' up the tents
And closin' all the trailers down,
It was time for the cards
Of the fortune tellin' lady to fold

And a couple roustabouts
Were out and making the rounds,
Waking drunks
And tellin' stragglers to hit the road.

She was standin' all alone
Out on them carnival grounds —
And in the light that was left,
She didn't look so old.

Well, I wondered if I ought to go
And talk with her,
Maybe even I could offer to walk back with her
To town, 'cause otherwise she'd go alone.

So I got up all my courage, actin' casual
Walked up like it was nothin' too unusual
But when it came to talkin'
My tongue just turned to stone.

Then I said, "Mary Jane Rae,
You prob'ly don't remember me;
You were a few too many grades ahead of me
In school —

I was just a kid back then, in junior high in fact,
But I admired you from afar
While I'd be sittin' in the back
Of Bus Eighty,
Which was on the rural route."

And you don't have to go home
All alone tonight,
We could walk together
Down the lane.

You don't have to let your own self
In tonight,
We could go a swingin' on the gates,
And then —

You won't have to let yourself
In tonight,
And you don't have to
Act out any age.

I could take your arm
And walk you home tonight,
And we could go
A runnin' down the lane.

She was standin' all alone
Out on them carnival grounds —
And in the light that was left
She didn't look like no old maid.

Trembling Field

R. Ryder Fawkes

This final selection of the *ANTHOLOGY OF NEW YORK STATE FOLK MUSIC - VOLUME ONE* serves as something of a preview and segue to the second volume, intended to be devoted entirely to the "lost album" (and, apparently, the only album) of the heretofore obscure R. Ryder Fawkes. While research on the liner notes of that volume is in progress, and further biographical information must await its release, suffice it to say that the artist was one of the perhaps hundreds of thousands of 1970's adolescents who, inspired what Dave Van Ronk referred to as "the great folk scare" of the late 1950's/early 1960's, penned Child Ballad influenced poetry and picked up a guitar - which, regrettably, he never practiced enough to learn how to properly play. *Trembling Field,* performed *a cappella* (and hence unmarred by the artist's otherwise substandard guitar work) is an outtake from the sessions that produced R. Ryder Fawkes' *STREET BALLADS* – slated for release as VOLUME TWO of the *ANTHOLOGY OF NEW YORK STATE FOLK MUSIC.*

Rare cassette release cover, © 1979.

Trembling Field

Oh, tremble, field fallow and dark
Where my love lay sleeping
Her heart press'd to my heart

Love, shiver, for soon we must part
Cold morning is nearing
Oh tremble, field fallow and dark

Her mother and father will know where we are
And the secret we're keeping
Her heart press'd to my heart

And the merchants count hours in the city so far
So we must be leaving
Oh tremble, field fallow and dark

Oh, flicker, f.ade the spread stars
In cruel light of morning
Her heart press'd to my heart

Love, shiver, for soon we must part
For morning is nearing
Oh tremble, field fallow and dark

Her heart press'd to my heart.

Willow

Tired, cold, I did not wonder
When I found the willow tree
In the wood, and left to winter
Felled, and split, and hardly green

Though snow blanked the forest
Kneeling with my knife I shaved
At the willow's heart for driest
Tinder to begin a blaze

Once, at first, a sudden spark
Flickered, but was quickly spent
Then I knew the willow's heart
Was not made of wood, but flint.

Since that time I have not wandered
To the willows, and will never.

Cornfield
with Crows

Russell Fox

Cornfield with Crows

Written 2013-2017 by Russell Fox
Buffalo, New York

Photographs by Russell Fox

Ancient Lights Books Octavo Edition Series #4
First Printing 2017

Ancient Lights Books

www.ancientlightsbooks.com

Cornfield
with Crows

By Russell Fox

ANCIENT LIGHTS BOOKS

Die Witwenvögel

There was once a farm on a hill where there lived a man and his old mother, a widow who spoke in German. The hill was crowned by a grove of hardwoods, ash and black walnut and oak, a *woodlot*. Below the high woods, rightward, a spread of tall grasses that had once been pasturage swept down and then leveled off at a red gabled barn with a round-bricked silo, the dome blown off and gone. Past the barn and the silo, farthest off, a white farmhouse stood at the edge of the place, facing away to the paved main road.

It was still called *The Sutter Farm* but there were no animals anymore and John Sutter did not farm it. Except for the farmyard between the barn and the house, where the widow had her garden, the farm was idle.

She was a small, spry woman. In the early springtime she worked her garden with an iron-bladed hoe, bent down and bonneted, her skirts to her ankles. She buried onion bulbs and the pared eyes of potatoes, and put in root vegetables and seedlings: turnips and rutabaga and parsnips and beets, cabbage and squash and radishes. At the far end of the garden, where she stooped to weed but did not till, she watched for the garlic and rhubarb and asparagus to come back.

Die Witwenvögel —

in a white skullcap with ties that ribboned under her jaw, and a man's wool shirt, checkered, and a linen scarf worn like a shawl about her shoulders —

with a birdbone pin for a fastening.

The farmhouse and the barn were on the highest land around. The broad descent of the hill was still parceled into lots by low fieldstone walls, limestone and rock that had been stacked in courses, but not cemented, more than a century ago when the fields had first come under cultivation. *Glacial shale,* that frostheaved every winter, and halted the plow and so had to be dug out and prybarred and sledged to the hedgerows, by *oxen,* and later by an *Allis-Chalmers* tractor, with spiked iron wheels. Until, in the next century, and within the widow's remembrance, the fields were abandoned, and the hedgerows were overgrown with scrub trees and wild vines, and the stone fencelines hid foxdens and woodchuck burrows.

The Sutters owned all of the broad hill below the farmstead, down to the ravine where there was natural spring and a creek, which was the property line. A wild old apple orchard grew alongside the creek, *cider apples.* Then the land lifted again, so that in the springtime the snowmelt off the hills flooded the creek, and the bottomland of the ravine became a marsh.

The upland across the creek had once been owned and cleared and farmed by *John Burke.* But all that property had been bought by an elderly dentist and his wife, named *Kaiser,* who were country neighbors of the Sutters. Doctor Kaiser and his wife lived in an old farmstead up at the crossroads of the paved main road and the dirt Burke Road, under the television towers. Except the small parcel for their house, the Kaisers' holdings were now rent land and crop rotated, annually leased to Ted Carley, who owned and operated a working dairy farm of more than a hundred cows at the bottom of the dirt road. Carley had cleared away the fieldstone hedgerows, from the creek up to the border along Burke Road, so that his great 4150 tractor could put in a single crop all across the rise, corn or wheat or alfalfa.

Ted Carley had never believed in buying much land, for tax reasons. But he had the right of first refusal on the fields he farmed, if the Kaisers were ever to sell any of it.

In the early spring of 1971, before the cut corn stubble on Kaiser's land had been plowed under, our father turned down the dirt Burke Road in his company car, a sedan, driving slowly. This first time was just before sunset on a windy late afternoon, and he stopped at the rise and got out and stood and looked back down the dirt road at the sunset, with the wind at that elevation blasting hard in his face, from the west. After that he always parked just over the crest of the hill, *to the lee,* and would come with two dogs, hounds. He let the dogs run while he stood out in the cropped field, hands in the pockets of his red mackinaw coat, with a hunting tag pinned to the back and the collar pulled up, hatless.

One evening he came with a dowsing stick and he walked with it until after nightfall, with the headlights of the parked car aimed into the field. He decided. Later that spring, when Ted Carley disked the land with the 4150 tractor, he left a rectangular acre of cut cornstubble in the middle of the great field, bordering the road. *Frontage.*

The widow Sutter and her son must have been surprised that the dentist and his wife had been persuaded to allot a mere acre of prime road frontage out of their holdings, and that Ted Carley had not exercised his right to match any purchase offer made on any the property. Later, from Dottie Kaiser, they would learn the name of the buyer, whom the widow Sutter would call *Fuchs.*

But he had personally called on the Kaisers, by appointment, and had made an offer. He was forthright, convincing; by profession a salesman in the foundry business, with big corporate accounts.

They wanted me for a neighbor. That's what it came down to.

181

✒

Now, it happened in that same early spring of 1971, when the snow was still on the hills, that a pony had got into the creekbottom. The pony was low and big bellied, with a shaggy hide of russet red-brown that was matted with thistles and burdocks. It grazed the carpet of thawed and rotting apples, wading the shallow marsh even after the seasonal thaw had flooded the ravine.

✒

Kinder

On a Saturday morning, after he had made the deal for the property, our father brought us all up there, to see it. His wife and two boys and his little girl. He led the way on a walk down the hill along the boundary line, an *acre*, pointing out the wooden stakes that had been pounded into the ground and flagged with plastic ribbons, the stakes spraypainted florescent orange. *And keep an eye out for arrowheads.* The Iroquois had lived and hunted in these high fields, and sometimes the arrowheads and even axe heads got plowed up in the springtime. *This is Indian land.*

We walked down to the creek and it was our sister who saw the pony first, excited and pointing. It was under the orchard branches, standing hock deep in the brightness of the flat cold water, in the milkweed and cattails and swale grass. Our father put his finger to his lips and motioned for us to stay on the bank while he waded out into the marsh, sidling toward the pony, but the pony spooked and plashed through the orchard trees. It climbed the steep bank in a sideways gallop and went through the hedgerow where the stone wall had tumbled into the ravine, and was gone.

When we got back up to where the house would be, he paced out the walls of the rooms in his old black army boots. Our sister just stood looking up to the fields across the creek, for the pony. But the fields below the farmstead were empty, greening with weeds and feral oatgrasses and goldenrod. The only place that the pony could have gone was into the tall forest at the top of the hill, the *woodlot*.

Ours would be the first of the new houses up there, a *ranch house,* with *cedar shake* siding and big picture windows overlooking the Carley Farm and the town in the flat valley far down below, to the *east,* the Town of Manlius, where we would go to school. All that summer, while the contractor was building the house, we would come along on the weekend trips up into the highlands south of Syracuse, to *Pompey.* The paved main road climbed *five miles* to our crossroads, which was landmarked by a tall television tower, to the right. There was a paved drive up to the tower, with a road sign that said *Sevier,* but the sign to the left said *Burke,* which was dirt and turned left off the main road and down into a narrow lane. The Burke Road, named after the farmer *John Burke,* was shady and dark, with fieldstone walls that were thickly copsed and canopied by apple and pear trees, down to where the road leveled out and the creek ran under it, in a steel *culvert.* Then the road climbed again, steep, and over the rise there was now our gravel driveway on the right, and a drilling rig standing off in the field, for the well.

For a few weeks there wasn't much up there except for the drilling rig and the gravel driveway, and the pallets of lumber and brick and tarpaulined bags of cement. Then one Saturday the foundation was cinderblocked all around and the groundfloor was poured with concrete, and then from week to week the house went up fast: the 2 x 4 skeleton, and the stairs and the plywood floors, up to the empty framing where the big picture windows would be. *Subcontractors* were brought in to lay the brickwork for the fireplaces, downstairs and upstairs, and to install the white *Romax* electrical wiring and the copper plumbing, before the walls could be *sheetrocked.*

The house was scheduled to be finished before September, when the year would start in the new school. But there was a problem with the well, which far into August had not yet hit water. On the weekends the contractors were gone and the drilling rig was idle and a decision had to be made whether to move it. The problem was the *elevation:* with the land so high up, there was no telling how far down the water table might be. The other problem was selling the old house, down in the suburbs. For a long while it wouldn't sell and the money for building the new house had run out. Even we children knew. It looked like the new house might not be finished until the next spring, if ever. This was when our father invented a board game, and sent the idea in to Parker Brothers.™ We never heard back from them. He took over all the interior painting of the upstairs of new house, while the downstairs remained framed and studded, without sheetrock.

But in late September, at 206 feet down, the drilling rig hit water. It would always be sulfurous, smelling of rotten eggs, and encrusting the sinks and shower stalls and the tub and toilets with yellow grit, but it was drinkable. *Potable.* And the old house in the suburbs sold, and there was enough money to finish the upstairs where the shag rugs and the kitchen and the bedrooms would be. And so, in late October we were moving.

To *Foxfield.*

As broke as he was back then, before the drilling rig hit water, our father bought the pony. The story is that he was driving down the dirt road in the early fall and had to stop for the cows in the road, which had broken through the fieldstone hedgerow and the electrified wire that was posted and strung along it. He got out of the car and was trying to prod and then pull the cows out of the muddy road, without much success, which is where and how he met Ted Carley.

Ted Carley could get the cows moving just by yelling *Yah!* and slapping a stick against his black rubber milking boots. He was compactly built, bandy-legged and barrel-chested, and he wore horn-rimmed glasses and almost always a baseball cap with the insignia of a seed company or a farm machinery manufacturer on it, because they gave away the baseball hats for free at the feedstore. It was a quick introduction between Ted Carley and our father, because the cows had to be herded back into the pasture, but once they were in and Ted Carley was re-wiring the fence, our father asked about the pony, which the farmer said that he owned, if anybody could claim ownership of an unbroken pony that no barn nor fence had ever held.

By now it was autumn, and the pony had moved up from the creekbottom and into the tall corn that was planted all around the *Foxfield* lot. Ted Carley, with a twinkle in his eye and a grin that didn't try to hide his conviction that his new neighbor would be getting more than he was bargaining for, offered to sell the pony, together with saddle and bridle, for *ten dollars* – on the condition that the buyer would get the pony out of his corn, and keep her out.

Somehow our father managed to lasso the animal, and dragged it out of the corn, and so when we moved into the house the pony was already there and tethered on a long rope to a stake in the yard, within reach of a haybale and a steel washtub that was big enough and heavy enough when filled with water that she couldn't kick it over (both of which, that first haybale and the tub, Mr. Carley had also sold him, separately) – a half-feral and shaggy and squat and big-bellied animal, which our sister had first noticed and called a horse but was really a *Shetland*, a pony, and which we knew was for her. The animal was named for the russet color of her hide, matted by the thistles and burdocks which our sister could never get it to stand still for long enough to brush out with the horse-comb –

Ginger.

In the mornings we were driven up the road and dropped off at the corner of the main road, to wait for the schoolbus. It was barren and windy up there, and so much colder than it would have been down in the wooded vale at the foot of the road, just past the Carley Farm.

We wanted to be left off down there. But no matter how snowbound and icy the road, every morning our father would make the sharp left turn out of the gravel driveway and take the steep hill, the car fishtailing when the road was icy. On the coldest days he usually would wait up at the corner until the schoolbus came, but sometimes he couldn't.

He went to schoolboard meetings, and spoke, but could never get approval for the bus to go down the narrow dirt road. If he started to let us off down past the Carley Farm, he said, then the school district would eliminate the stop at the top of the road because nobody else got on up there, and then in the afternoons we would have to walk up the road into the blasting cold wind, which was likely true. So every day the bus came up the main road and then turned around at the corner of our dirt road, which was the end of the route, because the Sutter farm, past that, had no children.

The schoolbus was something new to us, rowdy with rural kids of all ages, who were dropped off down in the town at the different schools. The quietest was a big kid with curly hair and full lips and a strong chin. Hobbes. Call him Tom. While he was still in early high school, Tom somehow got placed in a job as a sort of custodian at the nearby county park, where there was a waterfall. After that he was off the bus and disappeared for a few years, except for being seen up at the park.

But Tom Hobbes would also join the Pompey Volunteer Fire Department, which is how he figures in this story, in the end. The schoolbus has been written about elsewhere – as well as the kids on the bus, and much about Ted Carley – in my first book, which was fictionalized, and names were changed, but Tom wasn't at all in that book. Nor was this story, because I thought then that it all sounds too unbelievable, in print.

But this is a true story.

Great joke on us, which Ted Carley much later owned up to having at least suspected of the great bellied mare that had roamed the wide countryside, unfenceable amongst the corrals and pastures before being roped and tethered in our yard: Ginger foaled. A colt, more horse than pony, dusty brown and the progeny of Ginger, and so named *Nutmeg.*

Winter was coming, and this was before he put up the split-rail fence and had the pole barn built, so he needed a place to board the colt. Ginger had wintered outside before, and our father would have built some kind of lean-to for her, but a foal needed better shelter.

And so it was because of this that our father first met the Sutters.

Fuchs

Drove up, long driveway, and there was machinery running loud in the barn, so I walked past the house and out back to the barn. John Sutter was in there, trying to fix his Allis Chalmers tractor. That was the first time I saw him – he'd had half of his hand taken off, probably in a farm accident. I don't remember shaking hands, but it could have been his left hand that was maimed – I just don't remember, now. When I walked into the barn he was trying to get a v-belt on the tractor, onto a pulley, for the fan cooling system. To do that you have to have the tractor running, to feed and wheel the belt, which I had done too as a boy on the farm. I probably told him that – about your great-grandfather's Allis Chalmers tractor – and offered to give it a try. He stepped back. I flicked the belt onto the wheel with the palm of my hand – you always keep your fingers clear – and got it on the first try. He was impressed, but he didn't thank me. Then I told him that I wanted to talk to him about boarding the ponies for the winter, and he told me to go up to house and talk to his mother, and went on about his business.

She came out, onto the porch. I was never in the house, so I don't know about that. How they found it later. But she reminded me of my Grandma Huebl – kind, a gentle woman, small in stature. We arrived at a price – she set the price. She was good to the ponies, would carry down a bucket of warm water to the barn in the morning and at night, all winter. She had a way with animals, an understanding nature. When I came for the ponies in the spring she was out in her garden planting beans, and she had the beans in a pan that had warm water in it. She said that there was a benefit in planting a seed wet and from warm water, in the morning of a warm day.

Sad to see how things happened, after that. I got to know John Sutter, somewhat; I would drive us up for the town meetings, sit with him. In private he was quiet, soft-spoken, said hardly anything at all. But in public he got vocal, political. I don't remember what his politics really were, but he was a bitter man, excitable. Later he took to driving the streets of Syracuse in a truck, collecting junk on trash nights, and filled up his woods with it. All kinds of junk. And it got really bad after that, when his mother was gone.

On a bright, skyclear, springtime morning, our father led us out on a walk across the fields, northward, toward the Indian digs. *North*.

The geography always seemed upside down. Because *north* should be *up* the great hill, past the Sutter farm and beyond their woods, but it wasn't. Remembering, it could not have been. Because in the big picture window upstairs the sun rose in the morning to the left, over the Town of Manlius and our school, and in the evening the sun went down to the right, beyond the television towers, when you were looking up from our house toward the Sutter place. And so, by the sun, the Sutter farm had to be to the south. But it would always feel all upside down, where we grew up.

He led us across the roadside field, *north*, in his old black army boots and that Mackinaw with the hunting tag pinned to his back, the cornstubbled furrows muddy with wintermelt and clumping to our own metal-latch rubber boots, and then we came to the corner of two fieldstone hedgerows demarcating the next field northward – a great, square field that had been planted in wheat in the year before, and so was grassed and greening. And there, in the middle of that field, was a woodchuck, on its back, sunning its belly after a cold winter, in the midmorning warm sun.

He said nothing, but crouched us down and sketched the field with a broken sumac branch in the hedgerow's dead leaves: the field and its four corners, motioning to each of us. I was to reconnoiter behind the hedgerow at the far corner of the field, my brother and sister to the right and left corners, and then to wait for his signal. Which would be his hand held up, waved. We went out, he stayed. And when we were in position he held up his hand and waved, the signal, and we three children came out running and yelling and waving our arms and the woodchuck startled, and stubbily ran in an ungainly circle twice before heading toward the one corner of the field that was still quiet, until our father came out running and kicked the woodchuck with his steel-toed army boot, exactly under the woodchuck's chin like a hiked punt, the animal pitched high up into the air and somersaulting before it came down and hit the field, impacted, its neck broken and dead.

All this with nothing said, not a word. Our sister, who was crazy about horses, and collected figurines of them, pacing and rearing, knew when she was riding Ginger to look out for woodchuck holes, that they could break a pony's leg. And we two brothers, not even teenaged, had been checked out on the guns and were allowed to take his .22 rifle from the wooden gunrack, which he had made in wood-shop class in highschool, to go out to shoot woodchucks, if we wanted to do that. I don't know that either of us ever did, actually shoot one, though our brother became a trapper and I went out once, by myself, with the .22 and spooked a woodchuck close ahead and lumbering away, and didn't shoot. Spooked, too.

But our father was a hunter. He tracked and killed trophy bucks, stalked and brought down a bear once, and shot ducks and geese and birds. Partridge and quail. But his greatest kill was the woodchuck, with the three of us there for a tactical attack, no guns.

The wind, that day, was a slight breeze from the west. No scent of Man from the *south*, from where our father had waited for us to all run in, yelling. I don't recall what was said looking down at the woodchuck, if anything. Probably not much. We continued on into the hillocks and vales of the northern woods, which were big woods with log footbridges crossing creeks and streams, until we climbed to the crest of the hill where the Indian digs were, staked and strung into a grid of small plots by students from the university.

The owner of that land, then, was a surgeon, specializing in prostate cancer, with admitting privileges at the university hospital. In the livingroom of his modern glass house, across the main road and high in the pines, he had a glassed coffee table that displayed Indian remains, skulls and femurs and other bones. Irony: he died horribly, not many years later, of prostate cancer.

Cornfield with Crows

The Sutter Farm was maybe three-quarters of a mile away, *as the crow flies.* But you could see that it would be much farther to walk it, far afields – across the broad hill and down into the deep ravine, crossing the spring marsh and then climbing the hedgerowed fields up to the woodlot and barn. It would be quicker to walk up the dirt road, up to the crossroads under the television towers and then left, heading up the main road.

But that would mean getting past the house, and it would be some time before I dared to do that. First there was the abandoned farmhouse down the main road to explore, paintless and grayed by rain, with its walls stuffed with newspapers dating back as far as the 1920's and a cardboard Wendell Willkie campaign poster and the floors cluttered with the detritus of bottomless blue marbled pots and pans, jam jars, and lurid paperback books bridled by moisture and freezing and refreezing. And the barn beside that house, the roof fallen in, the handhewn beams and roughcut boards plundered by our father to finish the downstairs of our house, but the barn still with a hayloft. Some of the high school kids on the bus still remembered the children who had once lived there, shoeless in their summers, poor people. Before they left, they had pulled a boxspring over the open well, as country people used to do, even the evicted.

Then there were the television and radio towers. Both television towers, the greater and the lesser, had a brick building beside them, and there were cinderblock sheds at the base of each radio tower. The buildings looked uninhabited, emitting an electrical hum, and so it was a surprise to ring the conventional doorbell of the great tower building and to be greeted by a small man in overalls and a white t-shirt who was welcoming and pleased to show a country kid around the place, a dense little building filled with oscilloscopes and screens and banks of metal cabineted equipment. That wouldn't happen these days. But he was like a lighthouse keeper, lonely up there.

Our brother, meanwhile, was happy setting up his traplines and following streams and wandering the woods, taking the .22 rifle out into the fields. In his element. Up there, for me, there was only interest in where other people once had been, human civilization. Ruins of lost farms, the Indian digs, the handcranked rusted out waterpump atop a standing pipe down in the spring, the site of the old schoolhouse where there were still the iron sides of schooldesks under the tangle of overgrown sumac. Middens. For me, the untainted wilderness that our brother so loved was an emptiness.

And so it was only a matter of time before I went up the rest of the way up the main road, cutting into the field below the Sutter House, keeping low along the post-and-wire fenced hedgerow of the farmyard, then reconnoitering around the back to the barn. Up close to the silo flaking whitewash and then into the barn, under the low beams with still the rich smell of old trodden grain and, surprisingly, there were automobiles in there. Three old sedans, nothing classic, junked in there and tireless and not even cinderblocked under the hubs, spiderweb cracks across the windshields. Slashed upholstery, burgeoning with foam rubber, like scars. Radios, but nothing that could be pulled without tools.

And further into the dark barn, rows of iron stanchions. But not the tall stanchions for cattle, as down in the dairy barn at Carley's farm. These were to tether some other creature, and it was spooky in there, with dustmoted sunlight filtering in through the tattered roof amid those ranks of short stanchions, narrowly set and ranged into the farther darkness of the barn, which were a mystery.

Finally, the silo: crouching to enter the round tower through the chuted door at its base, the banded curved cinderblock unpainted inside, tall and roofless and empty but for a silting of graindust and, incongruous, at its epicenter, the dried coil of a huge turd in the dust, unmistakably human. Which, for some reason beyond words or reason, was scary, enough to make for a quick duck and dodge out of the silo, the barn, crouching in a run for the low hedgerows below the farm, out into the fieldstone bordered plots of wild alfalfa and grasses and volunteer wheat that had all gone to seed on the Sutter property. And looking up to our house beyond the marshed ravine, across the rise of broad unbroken field rented by Ted Carley, still unplowed cornstubble that early spring, the land was black.

With birds.

They were crows, a great flock of them, scrabbling for kernels of corn. And even after plashing across the cold knee-deep marshwater and out from under the crabapple branches, and climbing hands and knees and boots up the shallowed concave of the eroded and cliffed redbrown banks of the stream, and coming out into the field past the treeline amidst them, at first the crows did not move, except to keep at their furious scrabbling, even then. They flicked away and fluttered, making a path but staying as a flock to the broader ground, not yielding it, impervious until I came to the middle of the black field, where and when the birds became almost silent.

And then suddenly, and all at once, and as one, not startled but almost mechanically, like a single piece of machinery, the flock lifted in a cacophony of wings and cawing, and wheeled, and rose higher into the sky and flew off away in a black cloud toward the horizon, westward and across the hedgerowed treeline.

All this was like an omen, which even a child could sense, if not yet read. But that would come, in retrospect. And so, too, sometime later, the mystery of the short stanchions in the barn, when it had once been a working farm, would be solved, even before the creatures' desiccated graywhite skulls and leg and pelvic bones, unearthed from under a hedgerowed midden of rocks and stones, would confirm it: *goats*. The Sutters were Swiss, originally from Switzerland, where the language was German, too; they must have somehow brought their great phallused goats from the Alpine mountains, to raise them over here. *Die Ziegen.*

Woodlot

Sometimes at night we saw a fire up in Sutters' woodlot: a great enough fire to glow orange above the trees in the night sky. John Sutter, we said to each other, was burning trash.

Our father told us to stay away from the Sutters' property. John Sutter was *proprietary.* Our brother, laying his traplines, said that he always went around it, exploring the forest up east and southward of the Sutter Farm, and in the deep woods of the state parklands he had discovered a secluded pond and had made and marked a trail up to where the waterfall was, Pratts Falls. But during the summer he had trespassed up into the Sutter's woodlot, once, and saw something there, something strange, and told our father.

On a Saturday morning in late summer we started on a walk down the broad hill, planted now in wheat, to the creek, crouching under the tangled canopy of the stunted old orchard of cider apples, into the marsh clearing where there was the rusted hand-cranked pump stuck up on a pipe that had been hand-sledged into the babbling of the natural spring, probably by John Burke. Our parcel had once been part of the farm of John Burke, too, for whom our dirt road was named. All else we were ever to know of John Burke, who had left behind him no discovered house foundation or barn ruins or extant family, was that his name was black-painted into the lowermost pane of an old stained-glass window in the little white clapboarded Catholic church, up in Pompey. So John Burke had been a Catholic, like us, and a successful enough farmer to endow a church window. But whether his habitation had been down at the creekbottom by the pump, or even up alongside the road that had been named after him and where we had built our house, was unwritten anywhere and lost. *Likely,* our father said, *he planted all these apple trees.*

This far we had been. Now we crossed the creek, narrowed and shallowed at summer's end, the banks high and steeply eroded by the previous spring's melt and rains, all of us children following our father and climbing hand over hand by the protruding roots of the trees up to the edge of the embankment, where there was a low fieldstone wall along the property line, part of it tumbled into the creek. And then, past the creek and the stonefence and so past the property line, we hiked up the hill toward the woodlot. Hedgerowed fields of weeds, a few tall stalks of volunteer corn, and earless feral wheat. Until, three quarters of a mile away from our house, *as the crow flies,* we were at the edge of the woodlot. Looking around, there was nobody we could see watching from the barn, the house, anywhere. Our brother took the lead into the trees, *ash and black walnut and oak,* tall trees dense together and some of them standing dead, no undergrowth and a soft black loam underfoot, until we came out into a clearing in the middle of the tall wood, our brother pointing but quiet, whispering to our father.

What is that? It was a circle of thirteen large rocks, somehow dragged there and set equidistantly so as to make a circle, with a greater rock, flat like a table, *granite,* set in the center of this. But there was more. Staked outside the circle of rocks there was a wooden post, maybe a cut down telephone pole, painted *white.* And diametrically across from that, outside the arc of rocks, an identical post but twice as tall, also painted, *black.*

We children looked to our father, who perhaps almost immediately saw it for what it was, but was quiet. The long moments that he waited, hands in his mackinaw coat pockets and walking into the circle to look carefully at the great flat rock, were probably because he was making up his mind about whether to tell us.

This was deliberate, and took work to do, the rocks dragged into the woods, *probably with the Allis Chalmers tractor.* And then our father deciphered its symbolism for us. The poles were compass points, east and west, the posts painted white and black. Good and evil. The sun rises in the east, white and good. And sets in the west, at the finish of things, with black and evil. The maker of this mandala being a practitioner of black witchcraft, and maybe Satanism, though our father didn't say that. And at the center of it all was an altar, obvious to us Catholic children, but not an altar like the whitecloth covered altar over which the host was lifted in John Burke's church – or maybe it was. We went up to look at it, closely: no blood on its concave surface, but blood could have washed away in the rain.

We were told by our father, without needing to be, to stay off the Sutter property. After that we sometimes saw fire up in the woods, orange glow in the canopies of the trees, and one time our brother said that he had walked past the Sutter place at night and there were cars parked along the road and candles burning on the porch railings. And once, a couple of years later, hitchhiking home after a night down in the town, I was picked up by a longhaired guy and his girlfriend in a cotton skirt who were living up on the farm.

When you were a kid up there, hitchhiking was how you got around. Most people on that road you knew or got to know you, were regulars. They would pick you up whether you were shouldering a fishing pole or a hunting shotgun, no problem. The longhaired guy and his girlfriend were people I had never seen before, and never saw again. I had long hair myself, then, and the girl held up a joint and asked if I smoked, and I said *sure*, so she torched it up and passed it back, and when we got to the crossroads the guy pulled over at shoulder of the road under the television towers and idled the car so that I could finish it off with them. With all that, it seemed like I could ask about what went on up at the Sutter place, which is when they shut down. They looked at each other, quick glances, back and forth. Finally, snubbing out the roach in the ashtray and tossing it out the window, the guy said that Sutter was a pretty strange character and to just stay away from the place, and the girl turned around and told me, wild-eyed and maybe frightened, that all the walls inside the farmhouse were painted *black*. They were moving out soon, she said, and they both seemed too scared to be talking much about it.

That's all I know. I was gone before the fire happened. The story is that by the time the Pompey Volunteer Fire Department got there the house was fully aflame but that they got the widow out of the house, and that our old schoolmate Tom Hobbes (not his real name) walked her out on his arm to his pick-up truck and left her out there on the road in the shotgun seat while he went back to help fight the fire. When he came back, with the house given up to be burnt down to the limestone foundation, the widow was still sitting upright in the truck, as she had been when he had left her, but she was dead. *Perished.* I never heard where John Sutter was that night, whether he was there at all.

After that, John Sutter must have made foray after foray down into the city with his truck and wooden trailer, into each neighborhood on its respective garbage night, harvesting junk metal and discarded large appliances and dragging them into the woodlot – stoves & refrigerators & dishwashers & washing machines & driers & water-heaters – and hundreds of tires & oil drums – even foraging the curbside waste of the Syracuse hospitals, according to the findings of the New York State Department of Environmental Conservation, which upon his default in proceedings adjudicated in 1998 found that he had loaded up his woodlot with *regulated medical waste* and *construction and demolition debris* and *used oil in waste piles and . . . unauthorized used oil directly on the land,* and *more than 1,000 waste tires at the Facility* – which was never a facility, but a woodlot become a dumping ground with the ruins of that altar still there right there in the middle of it.

We were all gone by then: even our father had sold the house he had built – our mother having left years before and we children now having moved out, too; and our father, the last to leave, for up north to re-build the cottage that his parents had left him, which he had helped to foundation & carpenter & roof in the 1950's, previous to this story, previous to us.

He would say, later, that Die Witwenvögel was a good woman, that she reminded him of his father's mother, who emigrated from the Sudetenland, in Bohemia. Both were little women, who knew the benefit of planting a seed wet and in warm water, in the morning of a warm spring day, and practiced it.

Wiezenfeld mit Raben

The first thing a child wants to know upon the telling of a story is: *Is it true?*

Well, this is a true story. Look it up. John Sutter was defaulted and dunned $36,000 on 11/25/1998, pursuant to New York State Department of Environmental Conservation Case No. R7-0990-96-06, for the offenses described in the chapter above, and ordered to Cease & Desist from further environmental depredations.

John Sutter died on September 28, 2010.

I wrote about where we grew up in my first novel, as said above, but I did not then write about the Sutters and the sacrificial altar in their high woods, nor about the farmhouse fire or John Sutter despoiling his woods into a DEC agency clean-up site, because it all seemed to be too implausible for a work of fiction, as transmuted and fantastic as much of that book was. Nor did I write about our father, then.

Instead I wrote a book which was mostly true when it was about the farmer Ted Carley, who owned the house and the barns and silos and pasturage down at the foot of Burke Road, a working farm.

There were two framed aerial photographs of the Carley Farm high on the wall of the narrow Carley livingroom, where the couch and Mr. Carley's upholstered chair and the television were, just past the big square kitchen. The photographs were taken in the last days of the barnstormers, when an agent would come around to the farm with the flyover photographs of the property already taken and developed and enlarged to 16" x 20" color prints, suitable for framing, with the already glassed frames in the trunk of the agent's sedan. Ted Carley, like most of the farmers, who were justly proud of what they had cleared and tilled and cultivated, considered and bought. Mr. Carley bought two of them, which had color-faded into grayed green by the time that I was welcome in that house, home. Later I would see colored aerial photographs of the trench scarred country of the First World War, in France – green plaided hills with brown and yellowing tilled fields crowned with piney woods, and would think *how like the hills of Pompey.*

The pictures illustrating this story were taken after Ted Carley had passed, and after John Sutter was dead, but I did not know then that Sutter was gone. And thus it was with real fear that I trespassed again onto the Sutter property, long after we still owned land up there anymore, and had some kind of right to be there. The picture below is the driveway into the old Sutter property, a November day.

I got back in the car and turned and drove up Sevier Road, and parked over the hill under the television and radio towers, and got out and sat crosslegged like a kid on a big rock in the tall grassed field and smoked and watched the sun go down, red in the west. In the darkening hills, with the lights of the City of Syracuse spread across the flat expanse of Onondaga Valley below, like a starfield.

APPENDIX: BURKE ROAD & ENVIRONS

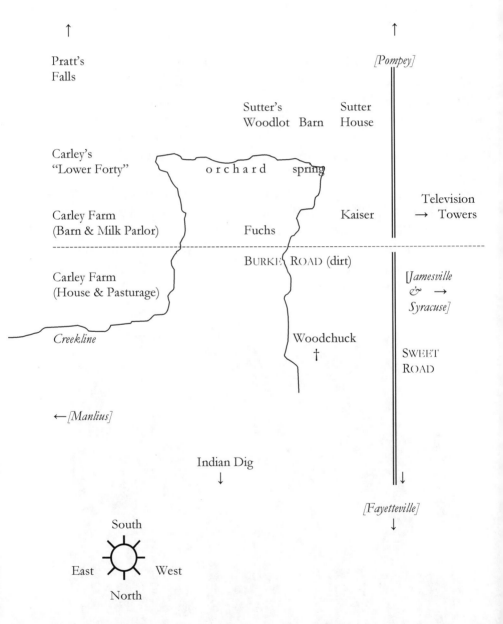

↑

Pratt's
Falls

Sutter's   Sutter
Woodlot Barn   House

↑

[Pompey]

Carley's
"Lower Forty"

o r c h a r d   spring

Television
→ Towers

Carley Farm
(Barn & Milk Parlor)

Fuchs

Kaiser

BURKE ROAD (dirt)

Carley Farm
(House & Pasturage)

*[Jamesville
& →
Syracuse]*

Creekline

Woodchuck
†

SWEET
ROAD

←*[Manlius]*

Indian Dig
↓

[Fayetteville]
↓

South

East   West

North

Burke Road

Long after nightfall
    years later
        And hearing the sound
        of pounding bare feet
        against the latesummer's dusk
        of rural dirt roads

And the pastures are brought to mind:

    The tangled trees of barren orchards,
    crumbled foundations, fallen chimneys,
    the abandoned wells, and rusted barbed wire fences;
    And the small cemetery, where smooth tombstones
    Are weathered almost illegible, bearing the names of local roads
    and are buried in the overgrowth of weeds and wild thorned roses.

Many nights I've walked these roads
filled with the smells of the granaries
and barns, and manure, and hay, and wildflowers.
Many nights I've heard again
the cows groan low beyond electrical fences.
And many nights since I've gone back to the barn
To swing from the loft
on ropes tied to rafters

Long after nightfall
    years later.

Sell This House in Winter

Sell this house in winter
When the snow covers the garden beds
We never weeded

Sell this house when the driveway sheets
Smooth with ice, and the broken pave
Is hidden

Sell this house when the roof won't leak
Or cellar flood, and the upper rooms
Are cold and clean and empty.

Blanket, sheet, and ceremented
Sell this house, this winter.

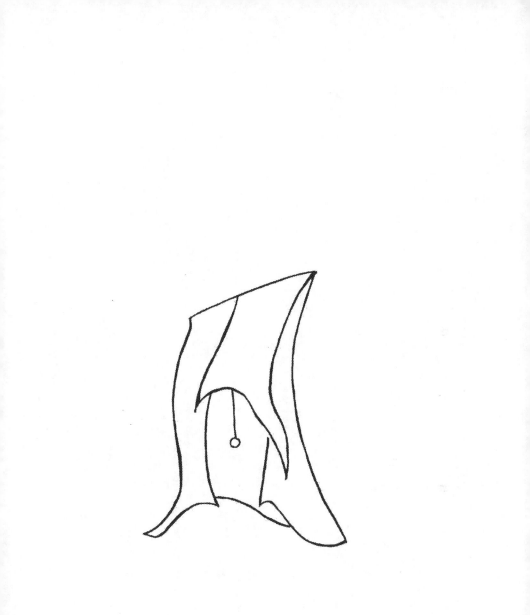

APPENDIX

The Very Last Dragon

A Problem Comedy by Russell Fox

Libretto & Score

Ancient Lights Books

The Very Last Dragon

A Problem Comedy, with Music

Libretto & Score by Russell Fox

Ancient Lights Books
www.ancientlightsbooks.com

Contents

Piano
March

Hark & Hail!

Russell Fox

Piano
Allegro

Extinctionary

Russell Fox

[Slow intro.]

Ex - hi - bit "A"; the great AUK, a dim-wit-ted, flight-less bird;

waddled sea rocks by the thousands while it was clubbed and massacred

[Uptick.]

This awk - ward and un - gain - ly AUK nonetheless had one distinction:

It was the first North American creature to be hun - ted to ex - tinc - tion.

6

© 2007

Piano
Allegro

THE VERY LAST DRAGON

Piano
Allegro

ORANG - UTANGS that still remain can now hardly be counted;

and the last PASSEN - GER PIGEON has been stuffed, handsomely mounted.

The QUAGGA of South Af - rica -- a Ze - bra head - ed beast --

like the RED WOLF in Amer - ica and STELLER'S SEA COW -- are deceased.

11

Piano
Allegro

and for al - most ev - 'ry creature   once we melt the po - lar caps

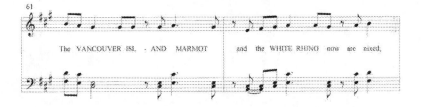

The VANCOUVER ISL - AND MARMOT   and the WHITE RHINO now are nixed,

like the defunct   Jamai - can monkey,   which was called the XENOTHRIX.

13

THE VERY LAST DRAGON

Piano
Allegro

The once-delicious YUNNAN BOX TURTLE in its shell sarcophagus.

is as dead as the ZEUGLODAN, ... whatever THAT was!

14

Piano
A battuta

The Rule of the Kingdom

Russell Fox

©2007

THE VERY LAST DRAGON

Piano
A battuta

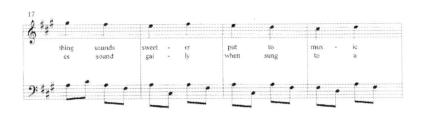

thing   sounds   sweet - er   put   to   mus - ic
es   sound   gai - ly   when   sung   to   a

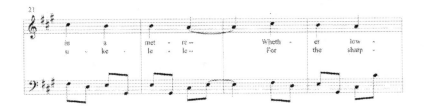

in   a   met - re ~   Wheth - er   low -
u - ke - le - le ...   For   the   sharp -

ly   grum - ble   or   the   high   de - mand.
est   barb   in   song   doth   lose   its   string.

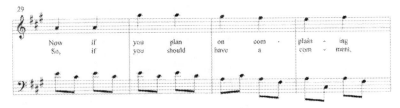

Now   if   you   plan   on   com - plain - ing
So,   if   you   should   have   a   com - ment,

17

Piano
A battuta

3

Piano
A battuta

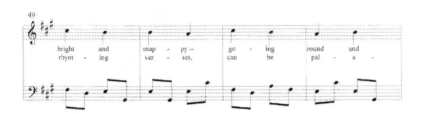

bright   and   snap - py ~   go - ing   round   and
rhym - ing   ver - ses,   can   be   pal   a -

round   in   end - less   roun - de - lay,
tab - le,   when   put   to   a   tune.

Piano
Vaudeville

The Breakfast Song

Russell Fox

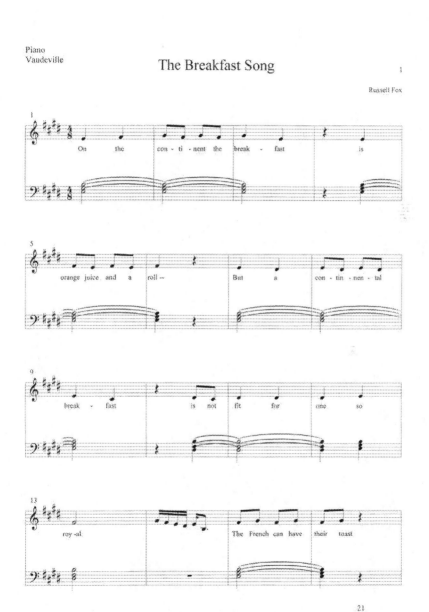

21

The Very Last Dragon

Piano
Vaudeville

with spice and su - gar sprin - kling -- Let the English eat boiled oats --

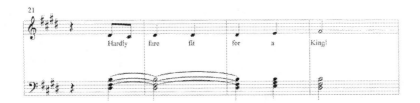

Hardly fare fit for a King!

But what is the break - fast for me?

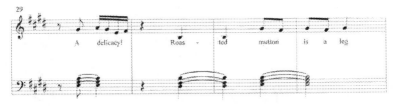

A delicacy! Roas - ted mutton is a leg

22

Piano
Vaudeville

Piano
Vaudeville

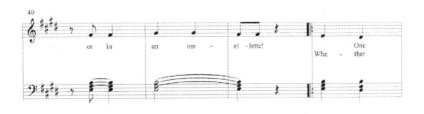

Piano
Vaudeville

5

What on Earth Could Possibly Go Wrong?

TOGETHER:	We don't have a worry in the world,
PRINCESS:	We're the freest spirits in the Kingdom.
TOGETHER:	If the world's an oyster, we're it's pearls,
HANDMAIDEN:	We're sweeter than two sugar plums, and then some.
PRINCESS:	I think tonight I'll wear this gold laced ball - gown ----
HANDMAIDEN:	It won't do to put just any plain old rag on ----
TOGETHER:	So ---- What on Earth could possibly go wrong?
HANDMAIDEN:	*(Spoken:)* But Mistress, don't you think----?
PRINCESS:	I shouldn't think so! No! ----
PRINCESS:	We don't have a worry in the world,
HANDMAIDEN:	Life's a bowl of cherries and a sweet song,
PRINCESS:	We're a pair of happy, carefree girls,
HANDMAIDEN:	For what we want, we never have to wait long.
PRINCESS:	No high-heeled shoes to catch the carpet shag on ---
HANDMAIDEN:	No sharp furniture for stockinged legs to snag on ----
TOGETHER:	So ---- What on Earth could possibly go wrong?
HANDMAIDEN:	*(Spoken:)* But, Your Highness, what about----?
PRINCESS:	What? But nothing! No! ----
TOGETHER:	We don't have a worry in the world,
PRINCESS:	We're the fairest flowers in the Kingdom.
TOGETHER:	People like to see us toss our curls,
HANDMAIDEN:	Except that sometimes people think we're ding - dong.
PRINCESS:	What a pretty hat ---
HANDMAIDEN:	But dear, you've left the tag on ---
PRINCESS:	How I hope this dance and dinner doesn't drag on ---

26

Piano
Sprightly

What on Earth Could Possibly Go Wrong?

Russell Fox

We don't have a worry in the world ---

We're the freest spirits in the King - dom,
Life's a bowl of cherries and a sweet song

If the world's an oyster, we're its pearls;   We're   sweeter than two sugar plums, and
We're a pair of happy, carefree girls;   For   what we want, we never have to

[3. People like to see us toss our curls;   Ex - cept that sometimes people think we're

then   some.   I think tonight I'll wear this gold
wait   long.   No high-heeled shoes to catch the car-

ding - dong.]

Al Coda

27

Piano
Sprightly

Down to the Dungeon

Piano & Bass Drum
Thundering

Russell Fox

Take them down to the dun - geon! Clap them in i - rons!

Let them just sit there and stew! Handcuff

and crack them! Shackle and rack them! Make sure you turn

ev' ry screw!

30

Piano & Bass Drum
Thundering

Piano & Bass Drum
Thundering

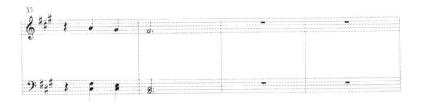

DOWN TO THE DUNGEON

KING: Take them down to the Dungeon!
                     Clap them in Irons!
                     Let them just sit there and stew!

                     Handcuff and crack them!
                     Shackle and rack them!
                     Make sure you turn ev'ry Screw!

HAL & BURTON: Down to the Dungeon!
                     Clap them in Irons!
                     Let them just sit there and stew!

                     Handcuff and crack them!
                     Shackle and rack them!
                     Make sure you turn ev'ry Screw!

KING: This *could* be a tragedy!
                     I need a strategy!
                     Crisis, catastrophe looms!

                     I need better surveil-a-lance!
                     Suspend habeas cor-p-us!
                     For toward us approaches our dooms!

HAL & BURTON: Down to the Dungeon!
                     Clap them in Irons!
                     Make sure you turn ev'ry Screw!

                     Handcuff and crack them!
                     Shackle and rack them!
                     Torture until they turn blue!

32

Piano
Lullaby

Bedtime Story

Russell Fox

The child-dren have knelt at their beds, their prayers are o-
ver now; And may they sleep, their souls
to keep ~ At least, un-til the mor-row. But the ghosts
still speak through heat pipes, if you listen in the night;

34

THE VERY LAST DRAGON

Piano
Lullaby

Whip-Song of the Errant Knight

Russell Fox

Piano
Emphatic

3

pro - duc - ton   o - ver - seas,   And pay   the help just a
we've picked their   pac - kets clean--   Well then,   we do it all

few   ru - pees!   And yen!   And pe - sos,   ru
o - ver a - gain!   A - gain!   A - gain   and   then

bles, yen!   And when   we need a dis - trac - tion--
a - gain!

Repeat ad
libitum.

That's when   we trot out the Dra - gon.

44

March of the Benighted Knights

Piano
March

2

17

woods are full of bears and wol - ves

21

hun - gry for a snackette!

25

All beasts of prey we keep at bay

29

by rai - ais - ing such a racket!

47

THE VERY LAST DRAGON

Piano
March

Flute & Piano
Affettuoso

The Ballad of Sir Shambles

Russell Fox

Ami   Ami⁷   Cma⁷

pp

There is a knight who rides da - ay and
oth - er knights look for dra - gons to

Ami⁷   Ami

night, and is known as the good knight, Sir Sham - bles.
smite, and they slaugh - ter the dra - gon that stum - bles.

Ami⁷   Cma⁷

And in an - y quest, he's the brav - est and
But Sir Sham - bles thinks that with dra - gons ex -

Ami⁷   Ami

best, and we'd ma - ny's the road that he ram - bles.
tinct, we'd miss how they make th' earth rum - ble.

51

Flute & Piano
Affettuoso

Like [To refrain # 3] all of the oth - er knights, he

went hun - ting for mean ug - ly dra - gons to fight;

and, af - ter the dra - gon he'd smite, th' eggs of

th' dra - gon he'd scram - ble. It

Flute & Piano
Affettuoso

Flute & Piano
Affettuoso

Dra - gon sang of its sor - row - ful plight, and its
Dra - gons aren't such an aw - ful bad lot -- true, they

song touched the heart of our er - rant knight; and Sir
thun - der and plun - der what men ha'e got -- but with-

Sham - bles sat down to con - si - der what's right -- and re -
out them ro - man - ces would have lou - sy plots -- and let's

solved to be some - what more hum - ble. Now the
face it, most peo - ple are numb - skulls.

54

Flute & Piano
Affettuoso

For dra - gons now are a spe - cies en - danger'd, they're ha - ted and hun - ted, fair game for a stranger. But some - one must cham - pion their cause, guard their mangers -- The Knight of the Dragons -- Sir Shambles!

The Platitudes

Russell Fox

Church Organ
Pomposo

58

THE VERY LAST DRAGON

Church Organ
Pomposo

Ex - cep - tion - al! De - fend we

shall! For free - dom is - n't free--

And the price that must be paid

is to The Hal and Bu - ur - ton Com -

Church Organ
Pomposo

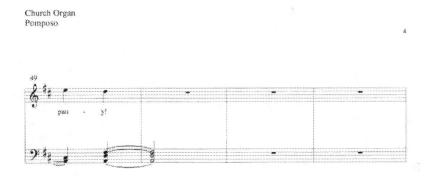

THE PLATITUDES

KING:
I am the Regent of this Land,
The Admiral of its Seas,
Defender of the Faith, commanding
All I oversee.

As Captain of the Ship of State,
In seas a-storm or swampish –
I stand this watch, and stand up straight,
'Til mission be accomplished.

HAL & BURTON:
As Captain of the Ship of State,
In seas a-storm or swampish –
He stands his watch, and stands up straight,
And mission is accomplished!

KING:
The fearsome Dragon shall not pass
Our flag shall never flag –
It's colors must hold hard and fast
And never run nor sag!

Exceptional! Defend we shall!
For freedom isn't free –

HAL & BURTON:
And the price that must be paid is to
The Hal & Burton Company.

Piano, Cello ad libitum
Aria

Princess' Aria

Russell Fox

61

Piano, Cello ad libitum
Aria

13
see something in its eye | old as earth and sky -- | an | un-der-stan-ding won ~ der
know deep down inside, | under that hard hide~ | a - | nother heart as vul - ner-

16
ful. | How | could I have nei - | ther seen nor heard,
'ble. | And | since now must be | the time of man,

19
but some ~ how al - | ways known; | what, | a ~ wa ~ kened to
to man I | must | a - vow: | That

22
a ~ wi - der world, | I'm touched and told | and shown. | So

62

Piano. Cello ad libitum
Aria

Piano, Cello ad libitum
Aria

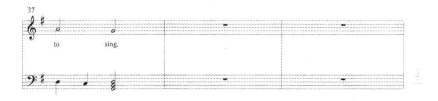

PRINCESS' ARIA

I
Never thought that I'd
Ever take the side
Of a thing so thunder full

But I
See something in its eye
Old as earth and sky –
An understanding wonderful.

How could I have neither seen nor heard
But somehow always known;
What, awakened to a wider world,
I'm touched and told and shown.

So my
Heart shall ere abide
Always at the side
Of this beast so blunder full

For I
Know deep down inside
Under that hard hide
Another heart as vulner'ble.

And since now must be the time of man,
To man I must avow:
That all this is something magical
Entrusted to us now.

64

Alto Saxophone & Piano
Andante

The Very Last Dragon

Russell Fox

66

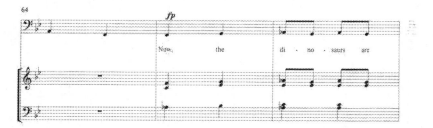

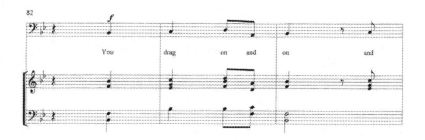

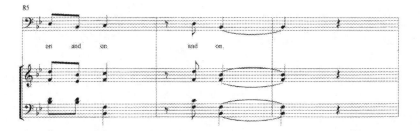

Index of Illustrations

All paintings, photographs, artwork and designs created by Russell Fox, except the following illustrations, which are in the public domain and for which copyright is not claimed:

Printed in the United States
by Baker & Taylor Publisher Services